Megan woke reluctantly from the most pleasant of dreams. In it, Reed Talcott held her in his arms. So realistic was it, so vibrantly sensual, that she could actually smell Reed's cologne on the sheet tucked up around her chin.

The sound of rain against the rooftop was wrong, the very light against her eyelids was wrong, as was the muffled twitter of house martins at the window and the texture of the mattress beneath her body.

Her eyes popped open in alarm. She stared at an unfamiliar ceiling. Abruptly, she sat up. Then she realized whose bed she was in.

Reed's bed! There was no sign of him, but she could see his clothes. She could see hers as well, folded neatly over the back of a nearby chair.

How had she gotten here? What had happened?

She was certain of one thing. It must have been a night to remember—if only she could. . . .

A Fresh Perspective

by

Elisabeth Fairchild

A SIGNET BOOK

SIGNET
Published by the Penguin Group
Penguin Books USA Inc., 375 Hudson Street,
New York, New York 10014, U.S.A.
Penguin Books Ltd, 27 Wrights Lane,
London W8 5TZ, England
Penguin Books Australia Ltd, Ringwood,
Victoria, Australia
Penguin Books Canada Ltd, 10 Alcorn Avenue,
Toronto, Ontario, Canada M4V 3B2
Penguin Books (N.Z.) Ltd, 182–190 Wairau Road,
Auckland 10, New Zealand

Penguin Books Ltd, Registered Offices:
Harmondsworth, Middlesex, England

First published by Signet, an imprint of New American Library,
a division of Penguin Books USA Inc.

First Printing, August 1996
10 9 8 7 6 5 4 3 2 1

To the Weirdos' Critique Group, who laughed in all the right places, and to my sisters, Deborah and Sarah, who pick themselves up and go on, no matter how many times life turns them on their heads.

ACKNOWLEDGMENTS

Special thanks to: Malcom Andrews for the inspiration I found in his lovely book, *The Search for the Picturesque* Jane Darnell, of the Cumbria Tourist Board, for specifics on mills, mines, and stone circles in the Lake District; and to Paul Doyle, of the University of Aberdeen, for the calls of the coot, warbler, and grebe.

Chapter One

The sight of Symonds Yat, ocher-tinted, through the lens of his new Claude glass, held Reed spellbound. Leaning his elbows on the window frame of the coach, he established a foreground on one of the elms that lined the road, carefully framed the copper green glint of the River Wye snaking around the base of the crag, and fixed the sky-raking bulk of the Yat itself asymmetrically on the horizon of his view.

"Do you know, Mr. Mollit, I believe the Yat is a worthy subject for a watercolor."

"The Yat?" Mollit yawned. Mollit had yawned often throughout the course of his tenure as Viscount Talcott's tutor. He had, in fact, just yawned his way through the wonder of Reed's first Grand Tour of Europe. The man's talent for boredom never ceased to astonish.

"Strange how I grew up in the shadow of this crag and never once did I think to paint it. It is only in coming back to it that I recognize its beauty. Strange! Do you not find it strange?" Reed did not wait for an answer. Any answer Mr. Mollit might make was bound to spoil his mood. Mollit had little appreciation or patience for the picturesque. Reed wondered if any sight had ever fired the older man's soul with artistic sensibility. Certainly none of the wonders they had witnessed in Europe had moved him. Perhaps all trace of the romantic had long since been expelled, along with Mollit's wind, in the exhalation of a thousand yawns.

"Teacher-teacher," the clear, ringing call of a tit from

the nearest tree, reminded Reed of Megan. Megan could mimic the call perfectly. She recognized beauty everywhere, in everything. He almost expected her to dangle bare feet from the tree as she had once been wont to do. Lord, how she would have been knocked breathless by the sights he had witnessed in Europe! How much nicer it might have been to examine the Sistine Chapel with the Nutmeg openmouthed with wonder beside him. Instead, he had been forced to endure Mr. Mollit, openmouthed, but not with wonder.

Reed sighed, his breath fogging the four-by-five-inch glass before his nose, adding a mystical beauty to the four-hundred-foot crag known as Symonds Yat.

"You do not intend to commit the thing to paper just this instant do you, Master Talcott?" Mollit's raised right eyebrow discreetly expressed his distaste for such a scheme.

"Paint it now?" The idea had definite appeal. Reed squinted at the sky. "No. The lighting is all wrong. Besides, Mother would have my head."

"As you say. Shall we proceed?"

Reed directed the coachman, "Drive on until you come to the bottom of the hill. I mean to stop at the rectory."

The carriage lurched into motion before Mollit could contradict him. Reed lunged involuntarily out of his seat, his knees banging Mr. Mollit's.

"Ow!" Mollit cried.

Reed's left elbow came down hard on the one crate he had insisted must travel inside the coach. Wood snapped. Sawdust packing material flew.

Concerned, Reed peered into the broken crate. No damage done. The bronzes had been carefully packed. He had seen to that. He held his Claude glasses—clear, rose, ocher, and umber, to the light for inspection. "Jove, that was lucky."

"Lucky?" Mollit scowled, nursing his kneecaps.

"Nothing broken. I should hate to have smashed anything this close to home."

They hit another rut in the road. Half the pile of ledgers Lord Talcott had entrusted to Reed in London slid from the carriage seat to the floor, banging toes, shins, and ankles as they went.

"Ow! Ow!" Mollit complained. "I cannot say I am at all fond of smashing things this close to home, myself."

Carefully closing up the stiff folio that protected his Claude glasses, each one framed in leather and conveniently hinged that they might be carried as one, Reed tucked it safely into the inner pocket of his coat. The lane always got bumpier in the last stretch toward Talcott Keep.

The rough condition of their progress meant that he was almost home. That pleased him. The ruts in the road, in an odd way, pleased him, too. They were the familiar. Reed had longed for the familiar of late, no matter that it might be an uncomfortable familiarity.

Mr. Mollit saw nothing admirable in the state of their progress. Like a disgruntled mole, he clutched at his spectacles with one hand and at the strap by the window with the other as they bounced through several teeth-rattling trenches. "I see your father has not seen fit to improve the roads during our absence," he said with a cough. Their passage raised a cloud of choking white dust that powdered them both, head to foot.

Reed nodded, blinking owlishly. He meant the move to be circumspect. As a rule, his movements were always understated and gentlemanly. However, as the coach lurched into another deep rut in the road at that very instant, his head jerked up and down as if he were a marionette and someone else held the strings. "Father rarely travels this way. He sees not the need for improvements."

"Lady Talcott cannot be pleased." Mr. Mollit had a talent for understating the obvious.

"No doubt," Reed said tersely. His mother was as

rarely pleased by his father's actions as his father was pleased to please her with them.

His tutor was frowning. "Neither will Lady Talcott be happy you choose to stop at the Breech's before coming home to her."

Reed shrugged—a gesture he had mastered in Italy. Reed liked the shrug and all that it stood for. He had taken care to master the movement with panache. He considered the gesture an appropriate indicator that he had reached the age of his majority, that he might now and again summarily dismiss the wishes of others. He patted the seven flapped pockets in his greatcoat, which bulged with small paper-wrapped parcels.

Another lurch of the carriage and the last of the ledgers slid from the seat. "Best leave them," Reed said as Mollit bent to retrieve the stack of books. "They are safer on the floor. Do you mean to step down? Or will you go on and announce our homecoming at the keep? I can walk up when I am done here."

"Yes, you can, young man." Mollit perversely continued to right the fallen ledgers. "I have no intention of getting down. I have not the energy, after such a trip as we have suffered, to face the brawling Breech clan. Why you should wish to do so is beyond me."

The coach slowed. The ledgers obeyed the laws of gravity once again.

"Ow!" grumbled Mr. Mollit, his efforts undone.

Subduing a smile, Reed stepped neatly to the ground before the books had resettled themselves. A barking beagle darted from the door of the honeysuckle-draped cottage across the road from the rectory. Three children followed close on the dog's heels, shouting, "Reed! Reed! You've come home! Mummy, Mummy! Reed is back."

Mr. Mollit was shaking his head and clucking his tongue in disgust as the coachman urged the horses onward. Reed knew he considered the Breech children completely lacking in discipline and manners. With Mr.

Mollit and the stinging flat of his ruler ready to leave stripes of reprimand in his palm, Reed had never been allowed to express such happy abandon as a child.

"How are you, Erin? Is that really you, Lottie? My, how you have grown. Have you lost a tooth, Cessy?"

Cecily nodded and grinned broadly that he might examine the blank spot. "A new one is coming in. See?"

"Let's have a look." He cupped her chin in his palm and examined the emerging tooth.

Three expectant faces smiled up at him. Three sets of small hands tugged at the tails of his greatcoat.

"What did you bring us?"

"Can we see?"

"Did you miss us?"

He smoothed Lottie's wayward curls out of her eyes. "Yes, I missed you, poppet. I have missed Blythe Corner and everyone in it more than anything else this past year."

"Are those our prezzies in your pockets?" Erin regarded the bulges in Reed's coat with unabashed interest.

"Indeed they are, Erin. Can you guess which pocket holds yours?"

Pointing gleefully, they dragged him toward the cottage, where Mrs. Breech stood watching. "So glad you are come home again, Reed."

"It is good to be home, Mrs. B." To his delight she kissed his cheek. Pressing one of the parcels into her hands, he emptied several pockets for the children. "Is Nutmeg in the back garden?"

"Where else? Go on through. She will be pleased you are home."

Into the house he went, into the welcoming smell of baking bread, roasting meat, brewing coffee, and the familiar rattle and screech of the budgie that hung in the corner of the parlor, greeting everyone who crossed the threshold with a squawk and the shrill admonition to "Look out for the cat. Look out for the cat."

David Breech came thundering down the stairs to pump Reed's hand and clap him on the back like a peer. "Hallo! Home again, are you?" His voice cracked on a wincing note. "How was the Tour? Was everything wonderful and strange?"

"Yes, marvelous and different. Everything different. I am glad to be back where nothing has changed so much as your voice." Reed laughed and stepped over the calico cat sunning itself in the doorway to the back garden.

"Dreadful, isn't it?" David blushed. "I sound like a broken bagpipe. The only compensation is that I've begun to grow a beard." He thrust forth his chin with pride.

"So Megan informed me in one of her many chatty letters." Reed squinted in the sunlight at the down that fuzzed golden the young man's cheek. "Perhaps this will come in handy."

Another present was plucked from the capacious pockets of his greatcoat. An ivory-handled razor with a fine Italian blade, emerged from the tissue wrappings. With an appreciative whoop, David set off to test its metal.

The garden was exactly as Reed remembered it: slightly overgrown, blowzy with roses, and beautifully still after the turmoil and activity that was always to be found in Blythe Corner, which was named for the Mr. Blythe who built the cottage rather than any state of mind one might expect to find within its walls. This garden smelled like England, the England he had been longing for. Reed paused a moment to breathe it in. This was the scene he had pictured, right down to the chatter of the robins and the cry of the cuckoo.

Down the winding path he trod, to the back corner where Megan had planted a cutting garden in a sunny spot, that the Breeches might always have flowers at their table. Megan was a dab hand when it came to growing things. At the edge of the flowerbed, she liked to set up her easel, to capture the ever-changing array of colors against the backdrop of the river.

Megan bloomed along with her roses. She stood at her easel, her hair fired with sunlight, the smock covering her dress as dabbled with paint as her face and hands were dappled with the light and shadow filtering through the elms. Reed paused a moment, took the enticing set of Claude glasses from his pocket, and held up the umber panel, that he might fix forever the image in his memory.

"Do not move," he said aloud.

Of course, at the sound of his voice, she did move.

"Reed!" His name caught breathlessly in her throat "Is it really you, Reed?"

She came running at him, filling the Claude glass, spilling over its boundaries. He snapped the leather case shut, slipping it into his pocket before she could knock it from his hand. Megan had not changed. Never still for a moment, her energy was boundless.

"Let me look at you." She threw herself and the familiar cloud of her tuberose perfume around his neck, that he might hug her and kiss her cheek. As swiftly, she pushed him away, her eyes bright with joy, or was it tears? "Are you changed by your Grand Tour? Did you bring back sketches of all the places you have visited? Do you mean to stay to tea? You must stay to tea. We have so much to catch up on and so little time."

Before he could answer a single question, she had thrown her arms around him again and was mumbling into the folds of his road-weary neckcloth. "Have you any idea how much I have missed you?"

Her enthusiastic embrace might have overwhelmed Reed had he not been used to Nutmeg and her ways. Her outburst pleased him. It was the welcome home he had anticipated. Her embrace was happiness itself surrounding him. He let himself get caught up in the warmth, even returned it with a hearty hug, a display quite uncharacteristic of him.

"Let me catch my breath," he said jovially. "You are

squeezing the life out of me. Yes, I am staying to tea. As for my being changed by the Tour, I have had quite enough of change. Every day has seen change this year—new vistas, new food, new hotel rooms, and new languages to deal with. Do you know that every time I asked for something I lived in fear of what might actually arrive? I am ever so relieved to come home to the familiar, to that which has not, and never should, change."

Megan let go her hold on him. "Oh, but, Reed, you are wrong. While you have been gone everything has changed."

Chapter Two

I am off on Monday," was how she began.

"Off?" He was not alarmed. Calmly, he settled himself on the creaky wooden swing that was tied to the lowest limb of the elm. He always favored the swing when he visited the Breeches' back garden.

"Yes. It was timely of you to stop by today. We have three days in which we must do nothing but catch up, unless you care to come with us. You never did write to say."

"Where is it you are off to?" He gave a languid push with his heels.

"The Lakes. You know. Gussie and Tom. A fortnight in a cottage. Nothing to do but enjoy the scenery and paint." She fairly sparkled with her happiness at the prospect. Her mouth, her eyes, her hands would not be still. Like the leaves above his head, she shifted and blew in the winds of her emotions. It had always fascinated him to watch her when she talked. It fascinated him now.

"Sounds lovely, but this is the first I've heard of it."

Her mouth dropped open. "You did not receive the letter? Do not tell me it is so. It was a very private letter. I do not like to think it has gone astray."

"Letter? I received a great many letters from you, Meg. A breath of fresh air from home, every one of them. To which do you refer?" Reed planted his feet firmly on the ground to still the swing and took the folio of Claude glasses from his pocket. He held one of the lenses to his mouth and breathed steam onto its surface.

"You do not know then, that Harold Burnham has proposed to me?"

The glass slipped from his hand, propelled by his abrupt exhalation. "Are you funning me?"

Megan laughed and clapped her hands together like a child. "No. Isn't it wonderful? Isn't it grand? I was never more surprised or delighted."

"You do not mean to marry him?"

Her attitude changed in an instant. All traces of the girl vanished. For an instant her expressive face and the articulate hands fell still. "Is there some reason why I should not? He is completely infatuated with me. Do you not care for Harold?"

"*You* do not care for him. Do not tell me you do. I will not believe a word of it. You are the one who told me that Harold's squint is characteristic of his very narrow outlook on life." Reed bent in the swing, picked up the glass, and fell to breathing on it again.

A pucker appeared between Megan's dark brows. "He is awfully nearsighted," she admitted, "but it was not very polite of me to point out the obvious. I cannot hold nearsightedness against every candidate for my hand, after all. Most everyone I know has trouble seeing some things." The pucker disappeared. A mischievous smile brightened her mobile features. "He is simply mad about me, Reed. I have never had the pleasure of a gentleman doting on me as he does. It is very flattering."

Reed polished at the glass with far more energy than the simple task required. "You've not said yes to him, have you? Not based on nothing more substantive than that you are flattered he has asked you."

She stilled again. Hazel eyes regarded him with what looked like reproof. "Of course I haven't. Do you take me for a simpleton? I would never do anything as flighty and foolish as that."

"What does your father have to say about this?"

She tossed her head, shining curls bouncing. "Oh, Reed. You disappoint me, you do. Can you not be happy for me, that I have received my first proposal? He got down on his knees and everything. I was sitting right there." She waved her paintbrush at the swing.

"Here?" He rose uneasily.

Megan was smiling as she daubed at her painting with a leafy green color. When had she begun to paint her landscapes in greens? She had been in the habit of favoring burnt umber and raw sienna, as he did, when last he had watched her paint. He crossed to the easel, that he might examine her creation.

"There is something very exhilarating about receiving one's first proposal, before one has even come out." She fairly preened. "I could not wait to tell you. I wrote you the longest letter, explaining it all in perfect detail. I knew you would find the whole incident as entertaining as I have. It is quite disturbing to think that of all letters, that one should go astray."

It *was* disturbing. All of it. Very disturbing. Even the painting disturbed him.

"You have changed the palette of your ground colors—even your brushwork looks different!" Reed felt dizzy, a dizziness that had nothing to do with the swing in which he sat down again to regard Megan as if he had never seen her before. Harold had proposed to her! He might have returned to find her married! The idea was too big to comprehend. "Do you really care for so much green in your landscapes? Have you given up the Romantic?"

"Yes. Having met the manner in which both Stubbs and Constable have used natural colors rather than the browns Claude, Rosa, and Poussin dictate, I decided it was time to try my hand at something different."

"Stubbs? Where have you met with this painter?"

"Not the painter, silly, but his works. We popped in on any number of Aunt Winifred's friends on the way to Paris." She said it as nonchalantly as if she were accustomed to junketing off to Paris every weekend. "One of them had a series by Stubbs, another a Constable."

"Paris?" He was relieved to see she was cleaning her brush of the green.

"Oh dear, was that in the missing letter as well?" She put down her brush. "Aunt Win took me to Paris for a week's worth of shopping. She has promised me a Season in London and insisted I required some fashionable attire."

"Did she? Decent of her." Reed was feeling strangely light-headed. A proposal! A Season in London! Even more alarming, these radical changes in her painting habits! It had never occurred to him that Megan might be transformed—almost as if an unseen hand had re-shaped her—in his absence.

"A blessing. Father calls her a blessing, and indeed, I agree. She has been the perfect angel." She untied the tapes that held her smock in place, revealing a pretty mulberry-and-white sprigged muslin dress he had never seen her wear before. It was cut in the new longer-waisted style that he had seen everywhere in Europe, with an exceptionally low neckline. Megan had acquired cleavage—attractive cleavage at that! When had her girl-ish figure reshaped itself? She was right. Everything was changed. She began to look like the dreadful bronze! He had yet to tell her about the bronze.

She whirled before him. "Do you like it? I have half a dozen more in every style and color you could imagine. New shoes, too, with little rosettes. Three new hats, one of them a leghorn that I kept trying to tell Aunt Win that I could not see around anymore than a horse can see around blinders, but she insisted on buying it. Told me it was the most fetching of the lot and would I like gloves to match! It is a good thing my aunt foots the bill. Papa could never have afforded such an extravagance."

Reed had polished the Claude glasses clean again. One by one, he held them up, first to examine her new style of painting and then to examine her new dress, new hair, and the arresting new curves of her body as she listed each item in her new wardrobe, her words flowing around them with the same graceful, rippling effect to be seen in the swirl of her skirts.

"I have evening dresses, three of them, a white court costume with a plumed headdress, a curricle pelisse with three capes, and a spencer with gabrielle sleeves." Her eyes sparkled with the wonder of it.

The ocher glass would not do. It left her flesh looking decidedly jaundiced while the umber glass gave her complexion a most unsettling bronze cast. Bronze! No, time enough to tell her about the bronzes. It was through the rose-colored glass Reed examined her at his leisure. She curtsied playfully, the girl he knew as Megan, who had become something more than the Megan of his memories.

"The color suits you," he said. The neckline did, too. He might once have said as much. The changes in her prompted him to hold tongue.

"Do you think so? I am pleased that you, of all people, should think so, Reed. You have an infallible eye for color."

"Your hair, it is different as well?" She looked taller, her manner seemed more confident. Was she wearing rouge? Or had he never really noticed the bloom in her cheeks? She had become a stranger of sorts, a fascinating stranger.

"Yes. It is the latest fashion in Paris and a great deal of trouble to arrange every morning. Mother likes it immensely. What do you think?" She looked at him as if it mattered a great deal to her what he thought.

Reed was temporarily at a loss for words. Megan did not normally fish for compliments or speak to him of fashions and hairstyles. Their conversation tended to center on more serious topics, like whether one should start from a burnt umber palette as the old school masters did, or the best methods for accomplishing a picturesque or chiaroscuro effect. How did one go about

sounding natural in giving compliments one was unaccustomed to offering? "I have always liked your hair. I
took to calling you Nutmeg in the first place because of
its wonderfully spicy coloring." His voice sounded too
harsh for the compliment.

She eyed him thoughtfully, as unused to hearing
praise from him as he was unused to offering it. "Did
you? I have often wondered."

"You have the look of a Boucher today, no, a Fragonard." There, that sounded better. The frog was gone
from his throat. It was true, too. She did remind him of
Fragonard's paintings.

She smiled, shy before him as she had never seemed
shy before, adding to his delight in looking at her
through the Claude glass. "I must paint you looking just
as you do today—just as you stand—against the backdrop of roses. I cannot imagine why I never thought to
do so before."

She would not remain still in the frame of his pictur-
ing. "What paintings have you seen? Tell me, tell me, so
that I may swoon with envy. But first, tell me what is
this you peer at me through? Have you purchased another Claude glass?"

"Yes. Smashed my round one on a mountainside in
Switzerland. A blessing really. I am much more pleased
with this new set than I was with the old."

"Let me see." She held out her hand for the folio and
carefully examined each of the glasses. "These tinted
ones are interesting. Where are your sketches? I must
see what you have done while you have been gone."

"They have gone on in the carriage, along with the
bronzes. I have brought back something rather special.
Can you come tomorrow, to see?"

A shadow darkened the sunshine of her smile. "Your
mother will not care to see me."

He laughed. "You will not be coming to see my
mother."

Chapter Three

Reed thought about change as he climbed the hill to Talcott Keep. After a year's absence, he had been prepared to surround himself in things blessedly familiar. Yet everywhere he turned there was change. It had started with the impudent Italian sculptor who had the temerity to take unforseen liberties with Reed's sketches he had been sent. Change had continued to confront him in London, where his father had dumped a stack of ledgers in his arms, saying he must look after his inheritance, they could no longer afford a solicitor.

And now Megan meant to go away for the summer with a Season in London hard on its heels and talk of potential husbands to take her away from him, perhaps forever. It was as if the world had begun to whirl on a new axis. Cresting the rise that afforded an excellent view of Talcott Keep, he wondered would there be changes here, too?

He slowed as he approached the crumbling pile that his Norman ancestors had called home in the fourteenth century. The moated castle was set within the original twelfth-century keep, hence its name. A Royalist bastion that had held off Cromwell's troops in 1646, its boxy, four-towered solidity staved off change with equal certitude now.

Through his Claude glass he observed the scene—umber this time. Talcott Keep should be seen through the smoky brown lens that added timeless antiquity to any scene. Oddly, it was not this place he had been homesick for during his European Tour. This was no Blythe Corner. Reed had never felt at home in Talcott Keep. It was too dark and imposing a setting to be comforting. It brooded too much over the past through keyhole windows meant to keep out the arrow-slinging enemies of Talcotts long dead.

The servants claimed the Keep was haunted. There were stories of a gray woman who walked the ramparts and reports of clanking chains from a dungeon no longer equipped with the instruments of torture that had once been housed there. The North Tower, dampest of the four, was no longer in use. Too much mildew, clammy stone, and rotting wood. If any part of Talcott Keep was haunted it must be there, Reed had decided as a boy. The place always left him depressed and dizzy.

He entered the castle, not by the formal great hall entrance, but by way of the low double doors that led to the buttery. He popped his head around the door to the kitchen to wish the staff, "Good day."

He was greeted with a chorus of polite welcome homes accompanied by a great deal of head bobbing and curtsying. Mrs. Daws, the cook, promised him a leg of mutton, minted peas, and Yorkshire pudding.

"You'll not have had any of that in your travels I'll be bound," she said.

"Quite right, and hungry for plain English fare I am," he pleased her in saying before he backtracked through the buttery to the great dining hall. Linen, crystal, china, and plate were being set out at each end of the long dining table for the evening meal. The glassy stare of a dozen or so stuffed deer racks artfully arranged between a score or more crossed arms above six suits of armor lent a martial air to every meal consumed. More head bobs and curtsies met Reed as he passed through the room into the main hall, where ancient family portraits looked down on him from whitewashed walls.

Another of the aging relics of bygone elegance and beauty, Lady Talcott met him at the base of the stairs up which he had hoped to escape for a wash and a change of clothes. She wore velvet, heavily gilded and lavishly trimmed. It was a rich, russet shade that echoed the coloring to be found in the tapestries that graced the walls, in the rugs at her feet, in the touches of rouge that enlivened her pale cheeks, and in the fur of the Pomeranian she carried everywhere with her. She had a fondness for the color. She had a passion, too, for velvet. It softened the ravages of time. Or so she believed. Reed's impression was that it softened the sound of her approach. His mother did not so much inhabit Talcott Keep as she haunted it. Tidbit, the chestnut-colored Pom who perched regally among the velvet flounces, seemed the most lively aspect of her presence until she spoke.

"So you come home at last, do you?" Her voice, like the French perfume that hung about her in an expensive fog, was penetrating, pervasive, and overbearing. Reed had learned the subtleties of his mother's moods through a lifetime of listening. Today there was no subtlety about her bitterness, her recrimination. Tidbit made a harsh little growling sound, supporting his mistress in her indignation.

"I am pleased to see you looking well, Mother." Reed leaned over the grumbling dog to salute her raised cheek with a kiss, as was expected of him.

"Well?" she repeated the word with icy disdain. "I am not at all well. I have been suffering the melancholia these last three months. Dr. Roberts has given me three different potions to drink, all of them vile, a pill to swallow at bedtime, and a highly restricted diet. My life is a misery. You are cruel to think me looking well."

"Beg pardon."

"I do not know that I can forgive you, Reed, when you are so unnatural a son as to prefer spending your first moments home from a long year's absence, not in ascertaining the well-being of your mother, but in the company of that Breech girl."

"Have I kept you waiting? I do apologize."

"Unruly girl! Always laughing out loud in the common fashion. She is never still. I was amazed to hear she had received an offer from Burnham's eldest. What can his parents be thinking to allow him to make such a proposal? I am immensely relieved you have never taken it into your head to fall in love with her."

"Fall in love with Megan?" The notion gave him pause. Megan was the sister he had never had. To regard her in any other way, especially on this day full of unwanted changes, held no appeal whatsoever.

"Preposterous, I know. But, you have always flouted my wishes where she is concerned. It pained me to think she had undue influence over you, who will one day inherit the Talcott fortune."

"I hope she does not accept Burnham's offer. I do not think she loves him."

"Love? You would encourage the girl to marry for love's sake and her with no dowry and no better than average looks? You do your friend an injustice."

"I am sorry you should think so." Reed knew his very affection for Megan spawned his mother's animosity. What she considered best for Megan was always a matter to be questioned. "I see Father has not seen fit to send the funds necessary to repair the road."

"Ha. The road. Your father is a rude and selfish creature with neither love nor money enough with which to endow his loved ones—of which there would seem to be too many to count."

She referred to his father's unending line of mistresses, on whom he lavished a great deal of his time, attention, and liquid assets. So many had there been, so varied their backgrounds, that the women had begun to be referred to, by the less tactful among the *beau monde*, as Talcott's harem. Reed had no intention of discussing his father's indiscretions with his mother. His father, after all, was not the only one to entertain the type of companion who required payments of one kind or another. He concentrated on the subject at hand, the road.

"I mean to fix the road now that I have come into my majority."

Her brows rose. Tidbit growled in her arms. "Do you?"

"Yes. Father has given me the management of our finances. Perhaps I can see to it that our affairs are placed in better order."

"Finances?" She frowned. "How tedious of your father to waste your time with matters better left to his solicitor. How is my husband?" There was acid in the question.

"He seemed well enough," he lied. His father's color had been too high, his breath too short, and his waist too wide.

"Is he?" She pouted, an expression that may have been charming when Clarissa Talcott had been a younger woman, but which now seemed nothing more than petulance. "What a pity."

Tidbit was grumbling again.

"He sends you his regards."

"Ha!" She knew better. "He wishes me to the devil. You need not pretend otherwise. Nor should you try to convince me you do not try to curry favor with him, though why you bother I will never understand."

"I brought up the poor condition of the road."

"Did you?" For the first time since his return, she seemed keenly interested in what he had to say.

Reed frowned. His father's reaction to the complaint had puzzled him as much as his mother's interest did now.

"The road you say?" he had roared. "She'll not wring another bloody cent out of me for that blasted road. Here!" It was then he had thrust the stack of ledgers at Reed. "You look after the damned road. I wash my hands of it, all of it, and of her!"

"He said I might take care of it, if I was of a mind."

"Did he?" Her interest waned. "You must go and

change, Reed, before you tell me any more. I will not have you to table in all your road filth."

She sounded, Reed thought, far more motherly than usual.

Megan did not really like Talcott Keep. Crenelated towers, like gapped teeth against the sky, it was magnificent in a dour, brooding sort of way. Overawed by the place as a child, the castle and its keep had seemed too huge for her, its size doubled by the reflection of itself in the moat that damply guarded the northern perimeter. It still seemed too dark and windowless. There were virtually none moatside, only the tall, squinting, arrow-slit portculises and the smaller, murder holes through which boiling pitch might once have been poured. And yet, today her heart sang as she topped the rise that led steeply up to the Keep. Reed was home—home at last after his interminable absence on the Grand Tour!

Long-standing habit, borne in her childhood, when children were neither to be seen nor heard in Talcott Keep, took Megan into the castle by way of the servants' entrance. The buttery always smelled pleasantly of food rather than of the beeswax and oil lamp odors that permeated the rest of the castle. She passed into the butler's pantry, with its high, glass-fronted cabinets, a place that dazzled her as much now as it had when she was a child confronted for the first time with so many tiered shelves crammed cheek by jowl with beautifully polished, Courtauld silver. The crowning piece, in her opinion, was the silver centerpiece—a beautifully wrought garden scene, about a foot long, complete with picturesque bridges, temples, and follies. The rest of the castle might be draped with valuable tapestries, paintings, rugs, and draperies, but it was the sight of so much glittering and taxable plate that had convinced Megan in an instant that Reed Talcott's family was possessed of more wealth locked away in a pantry than she would probably see in a lifetime.

Today, however, the familiar odor of the whitening powder with which the silver was polished was overpowered by the smell of a particularly noxious French perfume. Lady Talcott was lying in wait for her on the other side of the door to the butler's pantry. She and the music master, a Monsieur Vincennes, were seated at the long, oak dining table, dwarfed by its terrific size, their whispers echoing from the white-washed walls and vaulted, oak-beamed ceiling. Vincennes excused himself with a scraping of chair legs on the flagstone floor. He was on his way from the room before Megan had accustomed her eyes to the lamplit darkness that pervaded every room in Talcott Keep.

"My dear Miss Breech, how good it is to see you again. How very grown up you are looking. You are here to see Reed?" Lady Talcott rose. She was not a tall woman, nor was she plump or big of bone and yet she had always struck Megan as a figure of such power that she filled far more space than her slight form accounted for. Her manners, speech, and welcoming ways were flawless. She was gracious in the extreme—always had been—and yet, Megan was struck, whenever she shared a polite exchange with the woman—and their exchanges were always polite—that beneath the polished veneer Lady Talcott was a cold woman who did not care for many of the things and people she claimed to adore. She certainly did not care for Megan. The dogs she carried—and there had always been a dog to be carried, though none of them were so favored for more than a year or two—had always seemed more honest somehow in the expression of their feelings. They had all been of the sharp-eyed, gruff-voiced, shrilly barking variety.

"You must be as pleased as I am that Reed is returned to us again," Megan said.

"Not for long, I fear."

"No?" Megan's hopes rose. Perhaps this meant Reed had informed his mother he meant to join her in the Lake District.

Lady Talcott smiled at her indulgently and linked their arms, as if they shared a common bond. The dog growled very low at the intrusion of Megan's hand on his territory. Megan feared for the safety of her fingers, but Lady Talcott ignored the animal and patted her hand, as though it were as much her pet as the Pomeranian. "Reed must soon leave both of us bereft of his company, my dear Miss Breech. He will marry, snatched from both our affections by the charms of some well-endowed female of his acquaintance, just as you are soon to be snatched from the loving bosom of your family and friends. I understand felicitations are in order!"

"Felicitations?" Megan repeated.

Lady Talcott stroked the pricked ears of her current favorite. The dog seemed anything but soothed by her attentions. He looked more inclined to snap at Megan than before.

"On your approaching nuptials."

Megan was surprised that Lady Talcott should have heard of Harold Burnham's proposal, much less remembered the matter long enough to congratulate her. "I have been made an offer of marriage, it is true, my lady, but you are too hasty with felicitations. I have yet to accept the proposal."

"Surely it is far too propitious an offer to be refused. Burnham is both titled and well-heeled. What more do you require?"

Megan smiled. "I like Harold. I have been flattered by his proposal, but I would be sure his affections are firmly fixed and not of a fleeting nature."

"Wise of you, my dear. Very wise. I have known many a man's interest to be all too transient in nature."

"Perhaps even more important," Megan had to admit, "I would be convinced that my own affections are drawn to no other."

"Other? Is there another from whom you hope to receive an offer?"

"There you are!" Reed's familiar voice was like balm to Megan's strained nerves.

"Here I am," she agreed, impressed with his timing.

He looked, as he always looked, the perfect gentleman. No matter where he went, no matter what he did, Megan believed Reed Talcott was never mistaken for anything other than a gentleman of quality and means. His clothing, his posture, his stance, his gaze, all bespoke the unruffled English gentleman.

His expression was carefully schooled to hide emotion, a face of serious reserve and tight-lipped control. An understated facade, Reed did not call attention to himself in any way until he smiled. Then the carefully controlled gentleman disappeared and the lighthearted boy of Megan's youth briefly made happy the serious cast of his eyes. There was a gentle sadness about Reed's mouth and eyes. They carried a depth of loneliness that smiles served only to diminish rather than erase.

"I have been commiserating with your mother over how little time we have left to spend in one another's company."

"Been telling her about your upcoming Season, have you?"

Megan smiled at him. Dear Reed.

"We speak of weddings," Lady Talcott informed him.

"Ah!" His brows rose. He pinned a vaguely worried look on Megan. "Who's to be married?"

"You."

"Am I?"

Megan smiled and nodded. "Someday."

"Ah! So I am. Not today. Today I have plans only to amaze you with my new bronzes. You will excuse us, Mother?"

He gently extricated Megan's hand.

"You mean to take Miss Breech to your private chambers?" Lady Talcott asked.

"She cannot see the bronzes, else."

"My dear Reed, you must remember that Miss Breech

is no longer a little girl. Her reputation could suffer were it widely known that she spent any length of time in your private chambers."

"Nonsense, Mother. Everyone knows we are the best of friends. I promise you I have no designs on Megan's virtue. Do you fear I mean to ravish you, Nutmeg?"

"Reed! Where have you learned such vulgarity?"

Megan sighed. She would have liked to answer otherwise, but it was true, Reed would never dream of ravishing her. His only passion was in his art and his maps.

"No fear whatsoever," she said.

Chapter Four

Megan said nothing until they were halfway up the stairs had lined with Reed's impressive collection of landscapes; four Claudes, a Watteau, a Fragonard, five Poussins, three Rosas, a Ruisdael, two Constables, three Gainsboroughs, and a Turner. "A breath of the outdoors to lighten the dark closeness of the wall," he called them.

"Your mother is right, you know." Her voice echoed against the cold stone.

Ahead of her, Reed kept climbing. "Mother is always right. In what respect is she so accurate that you feel compelled to point it out to me?"

"It *is* inappropriate for you to whisk me away into your private tower, without so much as another female companion."

He laughed, the sound warm and radiant in the chill dimness of the stairwell. "Do not stand on form with me, Nutmeg. I cannot bear that that, too, must change between us." He turned unexpectedly on the step above her and leaned in close to her face when she bumped into him. "Unless, of course, you think me so changed by my travels that you fear, after all, that I shall molest you in some manner."

For an instant, there was an unfamiliar intensity in his expression. Megan's heart beat faster. He was leering at her! She shoved at him. He was leering at her in ludicrous lampoon of what he believed a rake must look like.

"Would Burnham call me out if I did?"

She was not amused. "Do not make fun about such a thing. It does not become you."

"Can I no longer make you laugh?" he teased and grasped her arm when she refused to so much as smile, his smile trading. "Do you think I have such designs in mind? Perhaps you do me the dishonor of confusing me with my father? For a moment you appeared to take me seriously."

"Nonsense!" She stared at his hand on her arm. Did he feel nothing of the charged heat his touch sent racing across her flesh? She could not look him in the eye. Of course he had no lurid intention in mind. She was not now, nor had she ever been an object of his desire, much to her regret. The love between them was completely one-sided. She had passed her youth with hope clasped to her heart, the hope that one day he would recognize the depth of her affections, would, in fact, reciprocate those feelings. In his absence, she had realized, when her aunt had promised her a Season in London, that her hopes were futile. Even if Reed Talcott did return her love for him, her world and his were forever separate. She lived at the bottom of the hill, he at the top. Megan Breech would never be mistress of Talcott Keep—not while Lady Talcott had any say in it.

How could he look at her so blandly when they stood so close to one another? Had he not the slightest notion how fast her pulse raced to have him home again and all to herself? There were no questions in his eyes when he looked at her, only the bland, unruffled acceptance that nothing was changed—no matter that time, and life, had passed between them. Megan's heart felt heavy—hopeless. She was more determined than ever to go to the Lakes.

Without a hint of the pain it caused her to admit as much, she said, "No, Reed. I know that it would never cross your mind to ravish any female. If it did, it would certainly not be me."

He nodded. "There you have it. No more nonsense about chaperones then. If you cannot trust me, who can you trust? Harold Burnham? Have you given him an answer yet?"

"No. We have agreed to discuss the matter of marriage when we meet again in London."

"He is in London?"

"Yes."

"Excellent. I shall have you all to myself until you leave for the Lakes."

Innocently clasping a hand that took hedonistic joy in his every contact, he led her up the remainder of the stairs to the room that was dedicated to his library. The room spoke in every inch of its space of Reed, in the books he loved, in the ordinance maps he marked with colored flags like a general mapping battle strategy as he kept track of what he called the encroaching hand of man over the land's natural beauty. A watercolor she had painted as a gift for him on his leave-taking hung above his desk. He had taken care to have it framed in his absence.

"How lovely!" She stopped to stare.

He thought she referred to the plush new rug at their feet in shades of blue, salmon, and gold. He dropped his hold on her hand as nonchalantly as he had taken it up. "The rug is not what I meant to show you." He waved in a cursory fashion. "Pretty though, isn't it? I had it sent back from Austria. The tapestry as well."

"Oh!" she breathed. "This must have cost you a king's ransom. It is the most beautiful thing I have ever seen!"

The scene depicted in the tapestry was of the beautiful son of a river god, Narcissus, languishing beside a mirroring pool of water, gazing lovingly at his reflection. Nearby, the comely mountain nymph, Echo, gazed longingly at her beloved, her body almost as transparent as the gauzes she wrapped herself in. According to myth, Echo had faded away, so desperate was her love, until she was nothing more than a voice. The subject matter made Megan uncomfortable. Like Echo, she pined for a man who was not equally affected by tender feelings.

But, fade away? Megan sniffed contemptuously and lifted her chin. She was in no such danger. Indeed, that was why she meant to go to the Lakes—though Reed was just returned. She would go to London, too, for a Season. She would wean herself away from unobtainable desires—not fade away.

"Never mind the tapestry." Reed crossed the room to the cabinets that lined the walls. "This is what I want you to see. Aren't they marvelous?"

A score or more bronzes, one of which he had picked up to cradle in his hands, were, as he said, marvelous. Each statuette was between a foot and a half to two feet tall. Superbly crafted replicas of Roman art, or originals done in the Roman style, each depicted the female form. Girls, young maidens, women, and goddesses—mythological and mortal, row upon row of miniature women captured in bronze. Youthful, supple, and lithe—happy or mournful, they were locked forever in time and metal. They gleamed with a rich, brown patina; every face, every hand, every ankle turned out to perfection. They seemed almost alive. Certainly they moved in the flickering candlelight. Together, they were nothing short of an altar to women—a gathering of graven images in which man might worship woman's every manifestation.

Rather overwhelmed by their perfection, Megan took the weighty figure Reed held out to her. It was Salome, draped in nothing more than a bronze scarf, eyes downcast, not out of any discomfort with her thinly veiled nakedness, but in a meditative manner.

"I wonder what thoughts so distract her," Reed said.

"One would hope she is questioning the wisdom of having obeyed her mother's wishes in asking Herod for the head of John the Baptist," Megan murmured.

"There is that," Reed agreed. The expression on his face as he regarded a statue of Venus pained Megan. That he might look upon a bronze female with more passion than she had ever witnessed in the gaze he turned in her direction—no matter that he held her dear, perhaps dearer than any other female of his acquaintance—left her feeling hollow, even jealous.

"She is perfect." Her voice was thick with unexpressed emotion. "They are all perfect—too perfect, perhaps."

"They are each of them gorgeous, are they not?" He caressed an Artemis, her arm tensed forever on the string of a bow. "Together, as a collection, they become something more. Don't you agree? The essence of woman captured for all eternity."

Megan felt defeated. These figures were too beautiful to describe the essence of woman. She had never met a single female who measured up to the yardstick these statues set, much less a score of them, all shamelessly bared so that their flawlessness might be admired in every detail. One by one, she examined them. In so doing, she felt she came closer to understanding what it was in women that Reed found attractive. In looking at the beauty and strength, the graceful symmetry of feature and form caught forever in bronze, Megan felt hopelessly inadequate. Her chances of securing Reed's love and devotion seemed more remote than she had ever before imagined.

"This one is for you." He held out to her a female figure with curling hair, a basket of flowers in her arms.

"Reed! How marvelous. This looks rather like that drawing you made of me. Uncannily so!" There was no mistaking the face, *her* face was on the bronze! It was the oddest sensation to see herself captured by a sculptor's hand. "It is your drawing! How?"

Reed watched her reaction keenly. A smile claimed his lips. "Do you like it? Do you think your father will have my head for this? You know, graven images and all that?"

Her expression serious, she pondered the matter. "I cannot answer for Father, but I love it!" She laughed.

"You have had me immortalized. A heady but thrilling experience." She could not take her eyes off the bronze.

His face lit with relief. "I thought the man captured your features remarkably well from the sketch I sent him."

So dear was this gesture of his affection that she all but forgot the statue in her hands. "You are so very thoughtful, Reed. How carefully you must have planned to bring something so special home to me." She wanted to throw herself at his neck. She wanted to weep.

His expression stopped her.

The lines of concern deepened between his brows. "I believed the thing well thought-out, but I have involuntarily kicked up a bit of dust. I hope you will see fit to forgive me the mess I have made."

"Mess? What mess?"

Reed chewed his lower lip a moment before grabbing up a crate in one hand and a stack of sketchbooks in the other. "Come, I'll show you."

He took her to their favorite painting spot. It would be easier, he thought, to tell her there. Yat Rock offered a marvelous view of the River Wye, slipping silver in the sun far beneath them. More than once they had brought a picnic lunch to this spot along with their paints and easels. Today they took no picnic, just his sketchbooks and the crate with one broken slat, from which a flurry of sawdust issued with every step he took.

The weather favored them with blue skies and sunshine. A few clouds, rare and unexpected masses of darkness passing above, momentarily blotted the light and the heat of the sun. The Yat smelled rich and fertile and green. A startled yellowhammer exploded from a volunteer private hedge as they passed—a feathery flash of yellow, chestnut, and brown.

"What is this mess you mentioned? You must not keep me in suspense for another moment," she insisted.

Reed was not sure how to begin. As if girding himself

for battle, he removed his jacket, rolled up his shirt sleeves, and set to work breaking open the crate. "The bronze I have given you was taken, as you guessed, from my drawing," he said. There, that was a start. "I sent it ahead, before my tour began, to a highly recommended Italian sculptor, asking him to have it made up for me."

"He did a fine job," she prodded when he paused.

He nodded. "That, and more."

"More?"

The crate successfully pried open, he reached into the sawdust packing and pulled forth a paper bundle tied in string. "Yes, if you will flip through the green sketch-book to the section where a page has been torn out . . ."

He paused in what he was doing to watch her reaction.

"Oh my," she gasped, her mouth a little O of shock. "Reed!" Her surprised gaze rose to meet his. Her cheeks were flushed. She spoke in a manner more rushed than normal. "I have never seen these sketches. They are not in your usual style."

"No." He felt rather like he had inappropriately exposed himself to her. He paused to collect his thoughts.

Megan had never been one to suffer silence gladly. She filled the awkward stillness. "They are marvelous, in a worldly sort of way. What a lovely sense of motion you have achieved here. The articulation of limbs is . . ."

He cut her off. "I thought them too provocative for you to view."

Her blush deepened. He had never before noticed how vulnerable she looked with pinkened complexion.

"Protecting the vicar's daughter again?" she teased with a pretty toss of her curls. "Do you find me so worldly you think I may now look on them without blushing?"

"No, I never intended that you should see them," he said ruefully. "But, given the circumstances, I've little choice. The thing of it is, several of the studies for these sketches were roughed out on the back of the sketch I sent."

He pulled from the nest of paper a bronze sculpture as he spoke.

"Oh my, Reed!" She could not contain her awe. As if the sketch had leapt from the page and gained form and substance, a pair of young lovers were clasped in a whirling embrace so fervent the bronze female was lifted from her feet, bronze skirt swirling around both their legs. Reed could not look at the pair without flushing. A spark of pure joy, of pure passion, seemed captured in the molded metal. He pushed his forelock out of his eyes. "Do you like it?" He could not contain his pride. He heard it spill into his voice.

Her eyes glowed with unadulterated wonder. "Reed! It is staggering in its perfection. You must be very pleased. Magnificent is too tame a word to describe the thing!"

He sighed. "My reaction as well when I first laid eyes on the pair. There is but one aspect that spoils my pleasure in the thing." He turned the bronze carefully in his hands so that she saw it from a fresh perspective.

She gasped. "Oh my! He didn't." She bent closer to be sure. "He did. The face, the hair . . . they're mine! Dear me!" Her gaze fled from the bronze to the sketches and back again before she looked at him in confusion. "Your sketches do not look like me." She flipped through the pages. "Not at all."

"Well no," he blustered. "*I* never imagined you in this pose. I never intended these figures should be cast, much less with your face incorporated."

She wore, for the fraction of an instant, a strangely disappointed look until her mouth opened on the thought of new horrors. "Have there been dozens made? Am I circulating all over Europe?"

"Well, no. I mean, there is only this one in my possession. The mold has been destroyed. There will be no others. If you insist, this *one* may be destroyed as well."

"Destroy it?" Her eyes were still intent on the sketches. He had devoted several pages to the figures:

arms, torsos, legs, faces, and hair. Was she frowning at the drawings, the bronze, or the idea of destroying it?

"I hope you will not insist," he blurted. "I have grown rather fond of the lovers. I even like the fact that the young woman looks like you."

"The lovers? Is that what you call them?" Eyes wide, she turned to gaze at him, as if he were a puzzle she wanted to solve. "I cannot be offended to find myself the object of such desire."

"No?"

"No. Every woman, no matter how proper her upbringing, holds a picture of just such rapture in her imagination."

"Does she? Does he remind you of Harold Burnham, then?"

She peered at the face of the bronze man. "Harold?" She laughed. "Goodness, no. I have never pictured Harold as the manifestation of my desires. This mystery man, however, is really quite splendid. I would hate to see him destroyed. It could, after all, be much worse. Your sculptor might have brought to life this creature instead."

She held wide the sketchbook to a page in which two more figures locked in passionate embrace. He could not look at the page. He knew all too well the male figure had goatlike feet and haired haunches. From the curling locks on his head protruded goaty horns. The female, her skirts whirling about their torsos as she twisted, was struggling, arms braced against the satyr's muscular chest, forever locked in a violent embrace from which she strove to be free.

He looked at her instead, willing her to understand.

Her eyes widened. Her hand flew to her throat. "He did not, did he?" She said it firmly, as if with the words she could stop him from proving otherwise.

In response, he drew the second paper-wrapped parcel from the crate.

"No!" Her voice fell to a whisper. "No! Tell me it is not so."

He could not meet her gaze as he unwrapped the bronze, the second of his sketches given all too solid a form and substance. "Believe me, Nutmeg, I would like to deny the existence of this thing, but as you see, I cannot."

He hoped she would not hate it too much. He could not hate it himself. Though it shamed him to admit he had a part in the creation of such a piece, there was something blood-stirring, even beautiful, in his rendering of a moment's savagery made three-dimensional.

She voiced his feelings perfectly in saying, "So alike, and yet so profoundly different."

He cleared his throat. "Yes. The dark, to balance the light side of passion. I visualized the drawings as a pair and the bronzes work together as such, but I never intended that you should be caught up in the pairing."

The words possessed a suggestiveness he had not intended either.

Megan was always a surprise. She surprised him now by laughing. It was a deep, throaty laugh, a flirtatious sound—as if she appreciated the double entendre of the words he had inadvertently chosen. "Of course not. I know you too well to suspect otherwise. However"—she laughed again, an almost hysterical sound—"my parents, if either of them were to see this work of art, and survived the shock, would insist on your castration immediately."

"Nutmeg!"

She had shocked him and seemed pleased to have done so.

"You think I jest? Do you forget I am the daughter of a vicar? This"—she waved helplessly at the statues and could not restrain another breathless laugh—"this scandal is one I could never live down were it to become common knowledge. There are already those who question my maidenly virtue due to the outrageous amount of time we spend in one another's company without benefit of chaperone."

"Who questions your virtue?" Her suggestion made him angry.

"Your mother, for one."

"Ah! Mother would. She questions everyone's virtue." Except her own, he thought. He shook his head. He must not be distracted. There was more bad news he had to share. "I have not told you the worst of it yet."

She was quick to guess the source of his concern. With an explosive laugh she said, "There is more than one of these, isn't there?"

He nodded, wishing above anything he might honestly tell her otherwise.

"Not dozens?" She sank down on the rock, her amusement completely uncontrolled. She stifled the noise of it only long enough to say, "Please tell me not dozens."

"Not dozens." He patted her hand, hoping against hope she would stop the hysterical laughter.

"How many?" He took a deep breath and blurted, "There were seven, but before you become too alarmed . . ."

"Seven!" she exclaimed. Laughter rocked her so uncontrollably she wept.

Concerned, he gave her hand a squeeze. "Four have been accounted for."

"Four?" She wiped her eyes and took a deep, shuddering breath.

"Yes, four. Two never left the artist's workshop, one I purchased from a gallery, and this one I chased halfway across Europe and bullied out of the hands of a Dutchman for an exorbitant sum of money."

"Reed!" Her voice was still amused—also forgiving. The sound of it closed his eyes with relief for a blessed instant. "Is *that* why you extended your trip?" She was chuckling now, her histrionics well in hand.

"Precisely."

"How very gallant of you." Her every word was a blessing and yet he still felt guilt-ridden.

"Least I could do, Nutmeg. I am only sorry I was unable to confiscate the three that sold before my arrival."

"Three?" She was the one to pat his hand now with a shuddering sigh that bordered dangerously on an outbreak of more laughter. "Well, it is terrifying to think there are so many likenesses of me wandering about out there, but far less terrifying than the prospect of seven."

She seemed determined to put him at ease. "What are the chances that any one of those three should fall into the hands of someone I know?" She asked the question rhetorically and immediately answered herself with an emphatic, "Incredibly slim, I should think."

Chapter Five

Did you really race across half of Europe to recover this thing?" The idea impressed her more than the bronze.

"Yes." He did not laugh. She wanted him to laugh. The whole dilemma would seem less frightening if only he would. "A dreadful chase," he said in so serious a voice she wanted to shake him. "We kept just missing the man. Mollit was no help and complaining all the way."

The very idea of Mollit in such a situation brought laughter bubbling to the back of her throat again.

"How I would like to have been with you."

"How I would have liked to have had you there."

"Did you miss me then?" she teased, hoping to provoke a smile, anything but the sad and serious line into which his mouth was pressed.

He shrugged. The gesture was new to him. To Megan it was one more sign of the unexpected changes Reed had, this day, revealed to her. That he had penciled such drawings as had since been formed into bronzes—that he should in any way express so much understanding of passions she had never dreamed him capable of feeling—astonished her. That he had so completely hidden a part of himself away from her was intensely intriguing. There was an unsettling hint of danger to it.

"Of course I missed you," he said. "So like are our tastes, so in tune our sensibilities, the whole thing would have seemed a grand lark if only you had been there."

But were they like? Were their sensibilities in tune? They should be having a grand lark now, given the humor of the situation. She took up another of his sketchbooks to hide her reaction, strangely saddened by his assessment and by his serious tone. They should both be giggling like children perched on the rock as they had so often perched in the past—hip to hip, shoulder to shoulder, his hands touching hers as the pages of his sketchbooks were turned from wonder to wonder. They did not laugh and she could not dismiss from her mind the sobering image of herself, cast in bronze, fighting off a satyr. She would never reveal the depth of her concern to poor Reed, who kept looking at her in the most pained manner when he thought she was not aware. More than the bronzes, she was troubled by the feeling that she was losing him, that she no longer knew who he was.

To hide her worries, Megan asked a stream of unending questions. She would drown her troubled feeling in words: normal words, average words, words that did not really matter in the grand scheme of things.

Reed answered her every question in detail.

Heads bent, one by one they examined his tight, accurate pencil, charcoal and conte sketches. There were written notes in most of the borders and an occasional watercolor like a splash of light and color, where Reed had taken the time to record his subject in the more liquid and time-consuming medium. The sketches their manner of transport, country by country, historic sight by historic sight, they relived the Grand Tour—Paris, Lyons, Calais, Venice, Rome, Florence, Naples, Geneva, and Brussels.

When they came to the end of the sketches, Megan leaned her shoulder against Reed's with a sigh.

"What an excellent guide to Europe you are! I feel as if I am just returned from a trip, not about to embark. Please tell me you mean to come to the Lakes. I cannot bear it that we should have no more than one day together before I go."

"You forgive me then, for unintentionally turning you into a lover?"

His words caught her by surprise. For a moment she could not fathom his meaning. She turned to gaze at his profile, hope flaring briefly, like a fizzling Roman candle, before she connected his comment to the bronzes he sat staring at.

"Oh! Yes. I even forgive you the satyr."

He smiled. Lord help her, she really must learn to control the lunging of her heart whenever his dimples flashed.

"Will you come? Please say yes. It has occurred to me that this may be our last opportunity for a painting tour together."

"Last opportunity? Don't be silly," he scoffed. "Life does not stop just because you are to have a summer at the Lakes and a Season in London."

She was frustrated that he did not see what she so clearly feared, even mourned. "Life as we know it is likely to change," she protested. "Augusta spent a single Season in London and returned to us engaged, with nothing but Tom and marriage plans on her mind. In a way, she never did come back to us."

"And do you think to find yourself a husband with equal alacrity?" He seemed amused, even skeptical of the notion.

Her chin rose in defiance of his lack of sensitivity. "If I should find a likely lad, or if I decide after all to accept Harold's offer, I would not at all mind being a married woman," she said tartly. "I am not so talented a creature that I may scoff at marriage and make my living with my watercolors. I have few other skills to recommend me to a life of spinsterhood. I am fully aware of the burden my continued presence may be to my father's purse. As I am very good at managing a household and garden on meager means, I think I will make some gentleman a useful wife."

"Dear God, Nutmeg! I never thought to hear you so

coldly discuss housekeeping and gardening as your only
reason to consider marriage. What of the tenderer emotions associated with such a union? What of love?"

She regarded him keenly—too keenly perhaps. He
had trouble meeting her eyes. Why was it, she wondered, that their friendship in itself was not enough to
satisfy her? Was she too selfish? She had thought about
her feelings for Reed for a year now. She had resigned
herself to putting a close to her foolish excesses of emotion. And yet, cutting off her love was far more difficult
than she had expected. The gentleness of Reed's manner
and expression drew her as they always had. The sun
touching the strands of his hair seemed more fortunate
than she.

She shook her head, trying to shake away foolish
thoughts. She must banish her desires. They would lead
her into trouble. She must stick with the plan she had de-
vised, to fall in love with another—someone sympathetic to her love of beauty, someone tolerant of her
painting. She meant to fall in love at the Lakes, or in
London. In fact, the idea of marriage appealed. Megan
had always pictured herself a wife and mother with
home and family of her own. That the husband she had
invariably imagined was Reed was the only part of the
picture that had to change.

"Love?" she said. "Of course I want love, but I cannot
go on expecting it to seek me out. I have decided to go
in search of it."

She waited, hoping he would contradict her.

He did not.

"Sounds a compromise to me." He evidenced no sign
of concern and she wanted his concern. She needed it.

She could not respond in kind. Words burst from her
lips almost without control, welling up from the heart of
her, shaking with emotion. "Life is full of compromise.
Every day we must make choices, many of them based
not so much on what we want or what we pictured, but
on what makes sense. Priorities must be set. We choose

what is worth our time and energy, our efforts and love. We turn our backs on that which does not fall into one of those categories. We turn our backs and go on."

"You would turn your back on love?"

"Love?" she exploded. "Again, you speak to me of love, when you have not the slightest notion what it is you refer to. Have you ever been in love, Reed? Will you ever let down the walls of invulnerability with which you surround yourself? How can you speak to me of love when you do not know the first thing about it?" She stopped the words that might have tumbled out— words that hung between them unsaid. *I love you!* she wanted to shout, to whisper, to cry. *I have loved you, adored you, cherished our every moment since the first moment I laid eyes on you. Do you know I lie awake at night thinking of you, longing for you to be near, near enough to touch?* Of course he did not know her feelings. He was completely blind to them, and she had never dared to tell. She would not tell him now. She bit her tongue and longed for recognition of her feelings. *I cannot go on this way,* she thought, *hoping, wishing, and dreaming of miracles.* It was a futile and frustrating existence.

"Do not speak to me of love," she said tersely. "You know it not! You know me not!"

She strode away, leaving him openmouthed and speechless.

He ran after her, of course, baffled by her show of temper. He was entirely unwilling to have the day end in so unsatisfactory a manner when she had taken the whole blasted bronze business so very well. Gathering up his sketchbooks, he tore after her.

"Nutmeg!" he called. "Wait. Please wait."

He caught up to her because she turned in her tracks, her expression drawn, her mouth ready with something to say to him, something so important she could not continue to walk away. He found himself almost afraid of her, this young woman he thought he knew in every way, who had proven herself and her feelings complete strangers to him.

"Megan"—he took both her hands in his and blurted before she could devastate him with more words—"you are quite right, of course. I don't know love at all well. Never did, until I met you."

Lips parting in surprise, her eyes lit from within, as if his words pleased her.

"Surely you know how dear you are to me? Why do you think I am always underfoot at Blythe Corner?"

She regarded him intently. He would have sworn she held her breath.

"Mine is not a loving home." He cleared his throat. Such a thing was not easy to admit. "I feel more love among the members of your family than my own. It should come as no surprise to you that I have yet to succumb to a grand passion."

Her expression changed. Her lashes fluttered down to hide her eyes. She looked for an instant disappointed. But so fleeting was the impression he thought he must be mistaken. After all, he had said nothing to disappoint, surely. To the contrary.

"But you, Nutmeg. I am surprised at you. You grew up surrounded by love and affection. How can you speak so flippantly of marriage? I must confess, it shocks and troubles me. I would not have you disregard so blithely something so precious."

Her gaze rose to meet his again, her eyes shining unusually brightly. "I do not disregard it," she protested. "I have, in fact, given the matter a great deal of thought. Far more than you will ever know."

"Because of Harold Burnham?"

He dropped her hands. There passed over her features, like a cloud passing over the face of the sun, the shadow of an emotion he could not read. She looked down, so that all he saw was the crown of her head as she asked him, her voice low and serious, "I know you do not think

Burnham is right for me, Reed. Tell me, who and what is right? What manner of man must I look for in marriage?"

He was uncomfortable with the question. He tried to shrug it away. She would not let him get away so easily.

"Please!" She looked up, her dark eyes serious. "I can think of no one whose opinion I might value more."

"What manner of man?" He began to circle, regarding her from all sides in a way it had never occurred to him to look upon her in the past. "Under whose care would I see you spend the rest of your life? Hmm." He began with the obvious. "A kind fellow."

"Kind?" She nodded.

He ticked a list off on his fingers. "Personable, intelligent, and easy to talk to. He should be someone of common interests with an understanding and appreciation of your many talents. Preferably someone not given to vices like smoking, drinking to excess, gambling, or whoring."

Her brows rose.

He refused to be anything but completely frank. "I would hope him to be a man of some substance and means so that you need not worry about money. Most important, he must be a gentleman bent on maintaining your own happiness as much as his own." He paused, a little unsure how to word his last recommendation.

"Sounds a splendid fellow." Her eyes sparkled with mischief. "Almost as if you have described yourself."

He laughed. How ridiculous. How typically Megan to cast such a suggestion in his lap. "I *am* a splendid fellow. You'll get no argument from me there, but I should like to think the man you marry will make your pulse race with anticipation whenever he is near."

"What makes you think my pulse does not race even now?" Her smile was enigmatic.

Used to her teasing ways, he made a move to grab up her wrist. "Shall we give it the test?"

She turned from him, scoffing. "You would not recognize a rapid pulse if you had it beneath your fingers."

Unwilling to be bested, he stepped in behind her, trapping her waist in the crook of his arm as if they were again children engaged in rough romps, and placed his first two fingers firmly against the pulse point in her neck. She struggled against his hold, gasped at his touch against her neck, and protested his manhandling by elbowing him smartly in the ribs. He let go of her, but not before the rapid beat beneath his fingers bespoke her agitation.

"Your pulse *is* racing!"

"Yours would, too," she said tartly, her cheeks aflame, "if you had been grabbed from behind like that. Do you mean to make me furious, Reed?"

"No." He opened his arms to her. "Kiss and make up?"

Her color deepened. "You treat me like a child."

"You're right." He sighed. "I do apologize, though I wish at times we might still be children." He ran a hand through his hair. "Can you forgive me?"

She took a moment, as if to consider the matter. "Not unless you promise to join us at the Lakes."

He smiled wryly. "You tempt me, Megan, indeed you do, but to make a promise I may not be able to keep would be childish indeed."

Chapter Six

Two days after Megan had gone, Reed was ready to race after her without a word to anyone. It was not the numbers swimming in his head and before his eyes, endless rows of sums explaining where his father's fortune came from and how it was spent, that tested his patience. He did quite well with numbers. That there appeared to be so much money squandered with so little to show for it, no more than made his head whirl. Silence could no longer drive him from the Keep either, though it had driven him as a child. Reed had learned to live with silence, to enjoy it for its meditative quality, to treasure the way he could focus his attention on whatever pleased him. He was focused today on the ordinance maps of Great Britain with which he had covered one wall of his study. It was absorbing work, absorbing enough he forgot for a while that Megan was gone.

There were a great many flags to be added. The landscape had changed in any number of ways while he had been gone. He had a stack of clipped newspaper articles to prove it. More riverways had been cut into canals. These he marked with wavy blue lines. Roadways, tollways, and post roads he marked with fat black lines. New industry, and there was a great deal of it popping up in the Northern Districts, were red flagged. Mines meant more flags: black for coal, gray for silver, and green for copper. Shale and graphite quarries were marked with two shades of blue. So much change in so little time! So many blots on the land. He could not spend an afternoon with his maps without feeling disheartened. But it was not an acre of new flags that so discouraged him this afternoon, though it did cross his mind that perhaps he ought to visit the Lakes while there was still some hope of viewing them in some semblance of pristine beauty.

It was, in the end, his mother's practice of chords and scales on the pianoforte downstairs that routed him from the Keep, armed with the ledgers, a sketchbook, and several pencils. Music did not bother him. It was the anticipated silence that would follow this music lesson that prompted his hasty exit.

His mother had always had the doting music instructor, or his equivalent. Dancing masters, music masters, voice instructors and language teachers—all of them male, most of them young, foreign, and handsome— each one favored by Lady Talcott's undivided attention and affections for about as long as the latest lapdog. Each one had taught Lady Talcott something new that caught her fancy, something that required long hours of practice behind closed doors—hours in which everyone, even Reed, had been denied access.

Lady Talcott knew the waltz better than anyone else in the district. She played the harpsichord, the dulcimer, and now the pianoforte. She could paint, after a fashion, cut silhouettes like a master, knew a modicum of French, German, Latin, Italian, Dutch, and a smattering of the Scandinavian tongues. She sang like a lark.

As a boy, Reed had discovered the real reason for his mother's many companions. It was in London, where they had lived for his early years in the company of his father, that Mr. Mollit had stopped him from rushing in to rescue his mother from suspected ill when she had cried out under the hand of a certain Monsieur LaPrelle, the French harpsichord instructor who came twice weekly.

"You must not go in." Mollit had stopped him.

"But Mama, she cries out, as if she is in pain." He had dared to question his tutor's wisdom.

"It is to Monsieur LaPrelle she calls. It is but part of the music lesson. I am sure of it."

"That cannot be. The music has stopped."

"There is more than one way to make music."

Mollit's innuendo had sailed right over Reed's head. It met with keener understanding from his father, who had chanced to walk in the door at the beginning of their conversation. Striding roughly past them, he flung open the door to the music room. A startled gasp met his entry. Looking in, Reed could see that his mother's music instruction was being conducted on the fainting couch tucked into the corner of the room behind the harpsichord, and that it in some way involved his mother sitting in Monsieur LaPrelle's lap.

"Up the stairs with you, Master Talcott. Quickly now and no hesitating on the way." Mr. Mollit had jerked Reed roughly away from the interesting scene.

"What were they doing?" he asked as he was manhandled toward the stairway. "Were they playing a game?"

"A game you'll know all too soon, young man. Up to your room with you. Make haste." Mollit had made sure he was on his way smartly up the stairs before he turned to go down, toward the servants' quarters, which were sure to be abuzz that the master had come in so unexpectedly.

Reed never did make it all the way up the stairs. He was stopped by his father's shout below.

"Out of my house!"

The music master stumbled out of the door red-faced and disarrayed, his waistcoat buttoned lopsided.

Heated words were quite shocking to Reed. Rarely were his parents to be seen together. When they were, so polite had their exchanges been that Reed had assumed them to be a happy couple.

He was, of course, mistaken.

"You, too, harlot. Be gone from my house."

"You mistake me, sir . . ." His mother's voice had floated up the stairwell, cool, collected, and scathing. "You mistake me, sir, for the common company you do more commonly keep. So taken have you been with a certain young songbird of late, that I did but seek to educate myself in the ways of music that must prove attractive to you."

Songbird? Reed had been intrigued. He had no idea that his father cared for birds, certainly not enough so that he would spend time with them.

His father, his face an unusual purple hue, strode from the music room. "How dare you, madam!" His voice had thundered in the stairwell. "How dare you bring this—this music master, whose dubious services I have paid for, into our house, that our son might learn such tawdry behavior."

His mother had maintained her cool composure. "There has been nothing in the least dubious about Monsieur LaPrelle's instruction or intention. The man's teaching technique might easily be labeled cocksure. As to exposing our son to the ways of the world, would you have me believe that he may learn such behavior only from his father? You would have to be here to teach him anything. As you are never here, rest assured he has not been influenced by his sire in one way or the other, unless it is to understand that your presence is not required either as a husband or a father."

"Am I even sire, then, of the brat you would have me leave my name and inheritance to? I begin to wonder, madam."

The brat, Reed had realized, flushing with shame, was himself.

"How I would love to spit truth in your face and say he is not, but you did your duty by me at least once, my lord. Reed *is* your issue. You do him and yourself disservice in classing him equal to the many seeds you may have spilled in other men's fields."

His father had looked up then. He had seen Reed

standing on the landing above—listening—face flushed and eyes wide with shock.

"Damn!" he had thundered, whirling on his heel to make for the door.

"We are not finished." His mother had begun to sound anything but collected.

"You are wrong, madam." His father's voice was taut with suppressed rage. The sound of it had frightened Reed. "We *are* finished, my lady, completely and irrevocably. I am off to sow more seeds, my dear, in fairer fields. You will, of course, remove your well-ploughed acreage from my house before I return."

The sound of the door slamming in his wake had resounded throughout the house.

More doors had slammed as his mother, in a tight-lipped fit of rage, bundled up their belongings. They had raced away that very night to Talcott Keep, the most remote of his father's holdings. Reed's contact with his father, from that day forward, had consisted of no more than an occasional glimpse. Far from his father's sensitive ears, Lady Talcott's music lessons had immediately resumed, with a thundering kind of vigor.

In time, and with feelings of shame, Reed came to understand the full extent of those lessons. He did not care to remain in Talcott Keep while they were underway.

He went wandering. Unintentionally, he went to all of the places he was used to going with Nutmeg for company. In an elemental way he could not recall experiencing so vividly since his childhood, he felt lonely. Megan's vehement insistence that she meant to marry, that things between them must forever more be changed by her going away, made more of an impression now than when she had spoken. He had lost something. Unaware, he had let it slip away from him.

He found himself unable to draw—impatient with the Claude glass and clumsy with his charcoal. He kept sketching faces instead of bits of the landscape. The faces were Megan's. Without Megan there to offer model for his sketches, his renderings were sadly lacking in the truth of what he was missing.

Closing up the sketchbooks, he turned once more to the addition and subtraction of lines of figures. Figures for food, furniture, artwork, clothing, and servants—figures for household expenses, for the upkeep of the animals, for his tour abroad. Figures, figures, figures. They kept his mind orderly, his feelings at bay. Sums for the purchase of new things and the mending of old. Sums for the rents that were gathered from adjoining properties. All of it was familiar, all of it consumed amazing amounts of money over time, most of it was mind-numbingly boring. Reed's eyelids had begun to droop when he came to an entry marked 'Repairs for the roads,' after which followed a string of dates and figures, none of which made any sense.

Repairs to the road? He sat up, shook the fog from his head, and stretched his back and neck muscles.

Repairs to the road? What repairs?

He broached the topic with his mother later that afternoon. "Mother, I have been going over the ledgers."

"Ledgers?"

"Yes, you may recall my mentioning them to you."

"What? The ones your father saddled you with?"

"The very same."

"What of them?"

"There are repairs mentioned. And sums of money spent . . ."

"Yes, yes?"

"Hundreds of pounds are listed, all designated for repairs on the road."

She fell silent.

"What road?" he pressed.

She sighed. "No road. I used the monies elsewhere."

"All of it? What for?"

She flung herself about petulantly. "This and that. Entertainments, Reed. Do not be tiresome and insist you do not understand. By claiming the money was for road improvements, I have been saved the humiliation of begging your father for funds he would not have given me otherwise."

It dawned on Reed that he had seen no sums listed for music, dance, or language instructors. "I see," he said.

"Your father?" Her voice was sharp. "Does he list his own . . . entertainments? Does he number them, or write them in by name? There must be a hundred or more lightskirts to his credit."

Reed studied his shoes and held his tongue. His father did have accounts set up to pay rent on five separate residences in London, only one of which he lived in himself. There was a staggering amount tallied to "Trinkets and Baubles," which covered God only knew what folly.

His mother paced the room. Tidbit, toenails tapping, skittered along in her wake. "This is really not your concern, Reed. I do not understand why your father troubles you with this kind of thing."

"Perhaps because I have just gone begging him for more money to repair a road he has already, according to the records, sunk hundreds of pounds into," Reed said reasonably. "I am concerned that our finances are not in better standing."

Her voice lowered dangerously. Her eyes narrowed. "Do you dare to pass judgment on me?"

"I have given Mr. Mollit notice."

He caught her off guard with the announcement. "Given Mollit notice? What has he to do with anything?"

"If my preliminary figuring is correct, we can no longer afford the man—no longer afford, in fact, a great many things we have taken for granted."

She set her chin, tossed her head, and sailed from the room, declaring, "Things are never as bad as that."

Wordless, Reed watched her go. Things were, he feared, far worse.

Chapter Seven

Lady Talcott's initially professed confidence that there was nothing to concern her was swiftly supplanted by anxiety. It carried her up the stairs, any number of times, to ask Reed questions he could not yet answer.

"I must look at the books myself," she said.

When the lists of sums were duly set before her, she eyed them through her lorgnette with a baffled look. "Explain what it is that I am examining," was her command.

So insistent were her questions, so frequent her interruptions, Reed could not think straight, much less finish his figuring.

"I mean to go to the Lakes," he informed her when he could no longer face her without gritting his teeth. "For a sennight. There"—*in peace and quiet*, he thought—"I shall finish figuring the books and return to tell you everything I know."

"Well," she huffed, "our situation cannot be as bad as you would have me believe if you are inclined to dilly-dally about the countryside with Miss Breech, rather than see promptly to our affairs."

It was with every intention of setting to rights the Talcott finances that Reed arrived in Grasmere four days later, travel-weary and no further along with his calculations. He found the cottage Megan had given him as address without any trouble. It looked cozy enough, but it was Augusta who offered warm welcome when the door was opened to him, not Megan, as he had hoped.

"Reed! How wonderful to see you. We did not expect you. Megan told us you were too busy to join us. I am so pleased you have changed your mind." Her greeting seemed, Reed thought, overly fervent.

"Where is Megan?" he asked when Tom went with him to the local inn to see to the disposition of his carriage and team.

Tom gave him a sliding, sideways look. "She and her new friends have ridden to Ambleside. A troupe of traveling performers are entertaining at one of the inns. They will not be back until midnight."

"So late?"

"Yes. Augusta will not say a word to Megan, but she is not overly impressed with what she considers the wild ways of this group she has taken up with. She has whispered in my ear a request that you wean her away from them if you can. You will have far better luck at it than Gussie, and well she knows it."

"Who are these people Megan has attached herself to?"

"Better you should experience them firsthand. I would like to hear your unbiased opinion of them."

Not another word was to be wrung from either of them. Reed was shown his room and then fed fit to bursting on Tom's catch of the day, broiled perch fresh from the lake. After a long-winded chat in which he caught up on all of Tom and Gussie's news, he retreated to the little attic room that had been designated his. By the light of the moon and two flickering candles, he played with the figures in the ledgers until his eyes watered with fatigue. Tucking himself into his bed, his mind turned over the trouble of his family finances as much as it toyed with the idea of Megan falling into bad company. He thought he would wait up for her, so restless was he, but in the end, candles burned out, he dropped off, only to be awakened by laughter, the nicker of a horse, and low voices.

He rolled out of his bed, cracked his head on one of the low beams of the angled attic ceiling, and stubbed his toe on something in the dark. Hopping and groaning, he made his way to the window, through which voices and a slice of moonlight filtered.

Below him he recognized the dark shapes of four horses and their riders. One of the shapes dismounted and helped a second to dismount.

"There you are, Signorina Breech. As promised, safely returned to your sister's care." It was a man's voice. He spoke with an Italian accent, rather sultry Italian at that. "Do your limbs tremble from having ridden so far?" He dared ask!

"Bloody flirt!" Reed murmured, rubbing his toe, but fully prepared to climb over the sill to pummel the man if he overstepped his bounds again.

Megan's response was a trifle breathless. "I am fine, thank you. It was a marvelous adventure, both to witness the farce at the inn, and to ride through unfamiliar country in the moonlight. Thank you for inviting me to accompany you."

"Our pleasure entirely," the Italian murmured. He appeared to bow over her hand to kiss it.

"Glad you could come." A female voice. "The players were so bad as to be almost droll, weren't they?"

"Shall I see you inside?" The Italian continued to test Reed's nerves.

Megan's laughter floated up to him, the teasing sound strangely foreign because it was another man who made her laugh. "An unnecessary kindness, Giovanni. Good night."

A chorus of good nights, and an outrageously forward *"Arrivederci, cara mia, buona notte,"* as the Italian remounted. The horses were turned. He heard the creak of the door below. Returning to his bed, Reed stared at the ceiling, his ears keen to the small sounds Megan made as she settled for the night. It occurred to him that they had never slept beneath the same roof before. The idea of it, combined with his memory of the scene that had unfolded beneath his window, disturbed him.

Cara mia, he had called her! How had Megan so quickly become this stranger's dear? And Megan, as if she had known the Italian for a lifetime, addressed him by his first name! Reed tossed about in the bed, more uncomfortable with his thoughts than with the lumpy feather ticking.

Sleep did not come easily to him that night. He rose later than was usual the following morning, happy with the anticipation of seeing Megan. On reaching the hearth, however, where Augusta and Tom were cheerfully toasting bread over the fire, he discovered that Megan, once again, was gone.

"She and her new friends have gone to the top of Helm Crag. There is a wonderful view of Grasmere Vale they mean to paint," Augusta said.

"Helm Crag? Where is that?" He hoped he did not sound as disgruntled as he felt.

Tom handed him a warmed piece of the local, flat oatbread and followed him out the door to point to the hilltop in question. "Gussie and I trekked up there with them at the crack of dawn. Megan required some help carrying her painting gear. Once they had set up their easels, however, we left them to it. Do you have a mind to head up there yourself?"

Of course he had. His whole purpose in coming was to see Megan, to sound her out on the recent turn of events in his life, to seek comfort, companionship, and advice. Reed grabbed up a second piece of bread, threw his sketchpad and pencils into a knapsack, and headed along the path Tom directed him to follow. He should have set a leisurely pace, lingering to enjoy the delightful countryside he passed through, but he was dismayed, even a trifle wounded, that Megan had gone off to paint without him in the company of strangers—one of them a seductive Italian. He hurried, and all of it uphill. His breath grew short. A stitch developed in his side. His pulse began to throb with unusual force in his temple.

Reed did not stop until red-faced and gasping he saw Megan. Contrary to his expectations, she was not surrounded by a company of strangers. She did, in fact, appear to be alone. His goal in sight, he pulled his handkerchief from one pocket, wiping the dampness from his brow with shaking fingers. With his Claude glass he framed the marvelous, glittering lake spread out beneath them. Megan, her back to him, her brush in motion, was his foreground.

"*Scusa!* You stand in my way." A melodic, masculine voice broke his concentration.

Megan turned. Gleefully she called out to him, "Reed!"

But Reed was transfixed by the sight of the gentleman who begged him to move. Like Giovanni Bernini's *David,* the man was sculpted perfection in the flesh. His hair, thick, dark, and curly, sprang from a noble brow, his perfectly proportioned nose and jaw seemed chiseled by a master's hand. His Cupid's bow mouth and thickly lashed eyes were almost feminine, so great was their beauty. Hauntingly familiar, it took Reed a moment to realize that the man was the spitting image of Narcissus, the son of the river god from his new tapestry.

The godlike creature was frowning—dark eyes, dark brows mobile—passionate in a manner that was anything but British. "No, no, Signorina Breech"—he passed paint-stained fingers through the springing curls of his hair, throwing them into romantic disarray—"you must not move. My painting, it is not finished."

"He's right, you know," a male voice again, amused this time and very English, wafted down from above them. "Foreground figures ought not to walk away in the middle of their rendering."

Reed's head swiveled. A gentleman and his easel, rather like a mountain goat, were perched on a rocky outcropping above them. His was not a handsome face. It was too long and angular, the mouth too wide, the nose too retroussé. And yet this fellow had an interesting look that compelled Reed to stare as much as he had at the godlike Italian. Perhaps it was his eyes. They were a piercing green. Perhaps it was his attitude. The man was completely at ease with himself and his surroundings, no matter that he perched precariously on a slender ledge. He exhibited undeniable poise and grace when he abandoned his painting and clambered down the rock face to regard the Italian's unfinished watercolor.

"He has captured the light well enough." He nodded approval. "But figures do not come easy to Giovanni. I, on the other hand, am a dab hand with figures who are overshadowed by atrociously muddy skies."

"Together you could make masterpieces," Reed suggested.

"There is more merit to that idea than you could possibly realize." The man smiled, the expression throwing the angular planes of his features into an arresting arrangement of light and shadow. "You must be the Reed who could not come." He held out his hand. "I am Richard Frost."

Megan was beside Reed then, tugging enthusiastically at his arm, crowing, "Reed! Is it really you? Have you brought your sketchbook and paints with you? Isn't this area absolutely divine? One could paint every day and never run out of new and interesting views."

"How are you, Nutmeg?" was all he had a chance to utter before she was introducing him, first to Giovanni Giamarco, whose resentment at having his painting interrupted might still be read in the brooding petulance of his expression, though he thrust forth his hand readily enough and wished him, *"Buon giorno."*

When Reed responded, *"Buon giorno. Che bella veduta!"* admiring the view in the man's native tongue, he warmed only a little.

Reed informed Megan he had already met Frost.

"Have you met his sister? Where has she gone, my lord?" she asked of Frost.

Reed searched his mind to determine which Frost this might be if he was addressed as a lord. "Are you related to Lord Frost, Earl of Banning?"

Richard Frost raised an eyebrow over one of his remarkable green eyes as if the concept amused him as much as it surprised Reed. "My uncle. And this is my sister, the honorable Laura Frost, who makes everyone question just how honorable she is by wandering off without informing her chaperon she means to do so."

Reed turned, with no expectation of encountering beauty, given Richard Frost's dearth of it, and was knocked quite unsteady by the vision of perfection that met his eyes.

Laura Frost was not happy with her brother's reprimand, but even miffed one could not mistake her for anything but a diamond of the first water. She arched a proud, pale, perfect eyebrow at him, her eyes the same striking shade of green as her brother's. It was the only way in which they resembled one another. Her face was as pale and unblemished as a perfect pearl, her features all gentle curves. Her nose was the only feature at all angular and it was so proudly aquiline one did not doubt for a moment that Laura Frost was honorable indeed. The rose of her mouth was the only color about her, save the green in her eyes. She had not the typically ruddy cheeks of the fair-complected. Her hair was heavy, straight, and blond, so smooth and fair a color as to seem almost colorless. She regarded Reed down the length of her regal nose, the depths of her eyes guarded by eyelids half closed. The world, Miss Frost's expression would have him believe, was a dreadfully boring place most of the time.

"Charmed," she said languidly, extending her hand regally, that it might be kissed.

Chapter Eight

Though she was not the woman he had come all the way up a mountain to see, Reed could not ignore Laura Frost's extended hand. Politely, he saluted it.

Lord Frost seemed not to care one way or another. He returned to his eyrie atop the rocks, scrambling up with as much grace as he had scrambled down. Megan, beyond a cursory welcome, seemed more interested in calming Giovanni, who made no gentlemanly attempt to disguise his distress at having his painting interrupted.

"A passionate man, our Giovanni." Laura Frost correctly interpreted the direction of Reed's gaze.

When he turned to look at her, she said smoothly, "I begin to believe he may be passionate about your Miss Breech."

"Oh?" Reed had suspected as much. He felt disappointed in his accuracy.

"Yes. His attention has been quite unshakably fixed these past few days." Her voice was soured by the faintest trace of irritation. "Are you bothered by the idea?" She eyed him quite keenly. "I am not quite clear just what the relationship is between you and—what was the charming endearment you used—Nutmeg?"

"We are friends."

"Only that?" She arched an exquisitely fine eyebrow.

"We grew up together."

"Ah! Platonic love? How very charming." She might have as convincingly yawned and said, *How very boring.*

"Megan is the closest thing I have to a sister," he said.

She had a mysterious smile. In a brief show of teeth it lifted her lips at the oddest moments. She smiled now. "I shall warn Giovanni. In my estimation, there can be no watchdog more tenacious than a gentleman who has adopted the position of sibling to a female, my lord. It is lord, is it not? Megan mentioned that you are titled a viscount, with a castle in Hereford."

Reed had more important things on his mind than pleasantries concerning Talcott Keep. Her words alarmed him. "Does this Italian require a warning? Is he bothering Megan?"

The flickering smile evidenced itself again. "Have I not just warned you, sir, that my Italian friend is a passionate man?"

Reed cleared his throat uneasily. "So you have." There was a hint of passion in the manner in which the honorable Miss Frost passed the tip of her tongue across the fullness of her lower lip, something that further substantiated the impression in the clinging nature of her arm, though her heavily lidded eyes still spoke coolly of nothing but boredom.

"And you, sir?" Her eyes narrowed, studying him. "What is your nature?"

Reed blinked. "I don't know that I am the best judge of that."

"Who better?"

She was flirting with him. He was not a complete stranger to flirtation. "Megan claims I am a romantic idealist."

A spark of interest fired in her eyes. "Does she? We shall have to see about that."

All Reed could see at the moment was that Megan seemed to have forgotten he was there. Her attention and conversation were directed to none other than the overly attentive Giovanni, who was, with far too familiar a manner, adjusting the tilt of her head.

When he would have interrupted the touching tableau,

the honorable Miss Frost diverted his attention by slipping his sketchbook free from his hold. "Do you mean to tediously devote yourself to drawing and painting like the others?"

"What? Oh, yes, I suppose I shall."

Giovanni brushed past him. "*Scusate*. You will be so kind"—he gestured broadly—"as to stand back out of my way. *Sì*?"

"But of course," Reed obligingly stepped aside. As he did so, Miss Frost snaked her arm through his. "You draw very well," she said with a cursory flip through his sketches. "There is a prospect not a dozen steps from here that you may find even more pleasing than the one before you." She nodded languidly at the view of Giovanni once again repositioning Megan.

Megan blithely allowed the adjustment of her shoulder.

Reed frowned. "Lead me to it," he suggested, acquiescent to the guiding pressure on his arm.

They did not go far. The view, no matter where one stood at the top of Helm Crag, was beautiful. Grasmere Lake stretched before them, light dancing on its waters and on the leaves of the silver birch and oak that lined its banks. Drawing forth his Claude glass, Reed examined the prospect with all due attention and respect. There was a calming effect to be found in a landscape interrupted by hills and mountains so little touched by the hand of man. Pulse slowing, his breath gentled, Reed's fingers itched to record the view in soft washes of watercolor. Neither charcoal nor ink could do justice to this view, though he whipped out his sketchbook and set down the line of the horizon with a few quick dashes.

He forgot the problem of his finances, forgot his concerns for Megan as she fended off the attentions of an Italian. He even forgot the lovely and honorable Miss Frost until a high-pitched feminine squeak startled him. Reluctantly he pulled his gaze from the Claude glass.

"Miss Frost?" he called out uncertainly and then with increasing vigor, "Miss Frost, where are you?"

"I have fallen." Her voice was faint.

He determined her direction and scrambled over the rocks that divided them. Poor Miss Frost would appear to have taken quite a tumble indeed. She lay prone in a crevice, shadowed by two great boulders, her skirt flung up about her waist in a froth of eyelet petticoats, her hair fallen down from its pins, a button on her bodice popped open to reveal far more than might be deemed decent.

"Dear God!" He felt close to panic. "Shall I give your brother a shout?"

"Help me, sir." She called to him, her voice weak, her hand beckoning.

Down the incline he went after her, an incline so gentle he puzzled a bit as to how traversing it could have so artfully thrown her among the rocks. Slipping off his jacket as he approached, he asked, "Are you injured? Does it feel as if any of your limbs are broken?"

Weakly, she lifted her head. "Oh my!" she quavered. "I am not at all sure in what state you find me."

"Don't move!" he directed sternly, covering her exposed bodice by draping his jacket over the top half of her. With a quick twitch of fabric he managed to make decent the delectable prospect of her exposed nether regions.

She sat up with far more energy than he might have anticipated, her expression one of dismay. "Do you not care, then, for the view, Mr. Talcott? I was sure you would find it enticing."

He thought her delirious. "Dear lady," he soothed. "Do not stir. You have gone all about in the head. Let me check first to see you have not broken anything vital before you attempt to rise."

She sank back. "Assess the damages then." She flung her skirt up, presenting shapely legs in beautifully clocked white stockings for his inspection. "I entrust myself completely to your probing examination."

Nervously, he eyed her limbs. He had never been given leave to stare so freely at a young woman's beribboned knees, much less to lay hands on them. "Very nice," he said. "I mean, you look just fine to me. Nothing obviously broken or cut. Your stockings are not even torn."

"Bruises, sir? Do you see any bruising? I am troubled by a prodigious heat in my flesh just here."

She took his hand in hers and guided it to a spot beneath the mound of her upflung petticoats, just above the tapes of her stockings. The skin of her thigh did seem warm. The heat was, in fact, quite contagious. He jerked his hand from her leg as if he were burned.

"You should probably expect some bruising," he suggested. "Do you have normal range of motion? Does anything pain you?"

She sat up and primly smoothed her skirts into place. "You are kind to ask. I am pained," she admitted, "right here." Taking up his hand again, she drew it under cover of the jacket he had flung across her chest and placed it with unmistakable purpose against the bared flesh of her breast.

"Miss Frost!" Shocked, he would have drawn away had she not held his hand beneath her own with such pressing firmness he could feel the beat of her heart in his palm.

"Laura. You must call me Laura if you mean to touch upon the pain of my loneliness, Reed. May I call you Reed, though we barely know one another?"

He nodded, unable to speak. Her behavior, while undeniably stimulating, was unexpected in a lady. He had been approached by whores with more subtlety in Paris, though he had not been at liberty to take advantage of their offers with Mollit always at his elbow. What was he to do now, with a young lady of quality offering herself up to him no sooner than they met?

"I should like to know you better," she said. "Much better. I should like for us to . . ." Her eyes, no longer bored, searched his as she gently guided his hand deeper into the bodice of her dress, that he might cup the soft swell of her breast. "Oh, yes!" She cried when he touched upon her nipple, which hardened beneath his fingertips. "Will you chase away my pain, Reed? I feel so very empty inside. Empty and lonely. Do you know what it is like to be lonely, Reed, desperately lonely? Do you ache with it, as I do?"

"Yes," he groaned, unable to deny the ache she had roused in him. That she should so swiftly recognize his need, that she should freely offer herself out of a need to assuage a loneliness that would seem to equal his own, drew him to her as much as the undisguised hunger in her eyes and the soft heat of her skin beneath his hand.

"Come. Kiss me, dearest Reed. Together we will fill the emptiness within and relieve our every ache."

It took every ounce of strength within him to refuse her. "My dear Miss Frost." He extricated his hand from its happy nest. "As tempted as I am to conduct myself otherwise, I cannot take advantage of your loneliness when you have just tumbled down a hill and may not be in complete control of all your faculties."

It was rather lucky he stood back from her in that moment, for none other than the lady's brother called down to them in that very instant. "Halloo! So this is where the two of you have gotten yourselves off to. What are you doing down there? Anything amiss?"

Heat rose in Reed's neck and face as he waved Frost down to them. "Yes. Your sister has taken a tumble."

"With you, dear boy, or without you?"

"She has come to no injury you will be pleased to hear."

"Has he the right of it, pet? Anything broken I should know about?"

"Just my pride," she said petulantly. "Reed could find nothing wrong with me." There was a trace of disappointment in the pronouncement.

"Nothing?" He laughed. "We are all flawed, Reed,

even my dearest sister. Perhaps you require a closer look."

"A closer look could not be had," she snapped.

Reed coughed, surprised she touched so close to the truth of the matter.

She went on. "He is, Richard, too much of a gentleman to point out the unwelcome truth if he has recognized any weakness in me."

"A gentleman indeed, to see that no harm should come to you under such provoking conditions." Frost slapped Reed companionably on the shoulder. "Your button requires attention, my pet," he gestured at Laura's gaping bodice.

"So it does." She glanced at Reed with a flash of the interest she had shown in him earlier as she languidly attended to the button.

Megan looked into the beautifully soulful brown eyes of Giovanni Giamarco as he knelt beside her, and understood perfectly why most women succumbed to his charm without hesitation. He looked at one as if he could remove every stitch of one's clothing through strength of sight alone. And in looking, he seemed completely pleased by what he saw. There was something undeniably exhilarating in the intensity and familiarity of such a regard.

"Alone at last, *cara mia*," he said sweetly in his deeply resonant voice "Long have I longed for just such a private moment with you."

The man was undeniably handsome. He spoke with a practiced earnestness that was almost, if not quite, believable. Why could she not be like other women and fall under Giovanni's spell? Her thoughts, to the contrary, were on Reed, who had no sooner met Laura Frost that he disappeared with her. That he should do so left her feeling hurt and angry, though she had no real claim to either pain or fury.

She smiled at Giovanni. He took her hand in his and

pressed it to his lips. "Do not, I beg of you," she said, "tell me that you are in love with me, or some such nonsense. You will find yourself much lowered in my estimation if you do."

The smallest evidence of a frown troubled his noble brow. "*Cara*, why should you not believe that I care for you?"

She could not help but smile at him. His was a pleasant, even an exquisite face despite the hint of petulance about the corners of his full-lipped mouth. He had the look of a beautiful child too long coddled.

"We have not known one another long enough for any declarations of that nature, surely."

His gaze passed slowly over the planes of her face, as intimate as a touch. It was an examination so comprehensive that it brought Megan to the blush. "So like," he said, "so very like. Your features . . ." He ran the tip of his finger along the curve of one burning cheek. "The promise of your sweetness has long haunted my dreams."

"Pretty words, Giovanni, but forgive me if I do not believe you."

"You do not believe me? I begin to believe you do not like me." He pouted.

"To the contrary. I do like you, but love is not so trivial an emotion that I will admit its presence where it has not had time to grow, much less flourish."

His expression changed. For an instant his true feelings evidenced themselves. She puzzled him, she saw. Perhaps it was curiosity that drew him to her. She had wondered all along why he would abandon the attractions of Miss Frost's cool beauty to evidence interest in her. His attentions had been undeniably keen from the moment he had set eyes on her.

"You do not know love." His words were a challenge. He softened them with the intimacy of a gesture, in which he reached up to smooth a stray curl away from her eyes.

"You are wrong about that," she said softly, sadly, her gaze drawn to the party of three that staggered toward them—Miss Frost supported between her brother and Reed.

"Ah! You are in love with him, no?" There was a hint of contempt in his voice.

"Yes," Megan admitted, looking away from the trio.

"And yet, he does not return your affections. He would not allow Miss Frost to lean on him so heavily if it were so."

She laughed. It was a harsh sound. "He does love me. As a brother loves a sister." She had never admitted as much to herself, much less confided the truth in someone else. How odd that she should pour out her feelings to Giovanni Giamarco, of all people. "It is all the love he has to offer me, I think."

"The man is a *buffone*," Giovanni whispered. "Has he no idea as to the depths of your feelings for him?"

"No," she admitted, tears welling in her eyes as she stared into the surprisingly sympathetic depths of Giovanni's. "He is completely blind to it. Has been for years."

"Ah, *cara! Non piangere.*" He wiped away the tear that spilled to her cheek very gently with the ball of his thumb. "Unrequited love. A tragedy of feeling, my dear. I do understand. Shall we make him *geloso,* how do you say, jealous? If there are feelings buried within him for you, there is no greater, surer prod than jealousy."

She blinked away the threat of another tear, straightened her shoulders, and forced a smile to her lips. "No. You are very kind to offer, but I will not stoop to lies and fabrication in order to win him, if he is not to be won. I have come on this trip, in fact, with every intention of severing myself from this tragedy of feeling."

"Bravo!" Giovanni's smile was contagious. She did not even bother to contradict him when he crowed happily, "There is hope for the rest of us in such a severing."

Chapter Nine

Very chummy they were, Megan and the too-perfect Italian, Giovanni. Reed wondered just how fast and how far the man had managed to progress his suite in the few days he had had access to Megan's unschooled ear. A rogue, by the looks of him. Up to no good. Megan was naive enough to fall prey to such a character. It was a good thing he had decided to come to the Lakes.

"Tell me more of your friends," he suggested that evening when they walked together to the lakeside in the gathering larch-scented dusk. Gussie and Tom strolled a few paces behind them, an uneasy reminder that Megan had reached an age when the two of them would find few opportunities to walk or talk alone and unescorted.

"What would you like to know?"

When he turned to regard her profile he was annoyed to find her features completely obscured by the dreadful leghorn bonnet her aunt had foisted upon her. It was black, lined with white satin, and edged in blond quilling and black ostrich feathers. Reed thought it looked like nothing so much as a decorated coal scuttle upended on Megan's head. He would have liked to buy her a more attractive bonnet. It was alarming to think he had not even enough money for such a simple frippery.

"How did you meet them?" he asked.

The coal scuttle nodded. "On a walk, such as this. Gussie had heard of a beauty spot in Ambleside called Stock Ghyll Force, a waterfall that is supposed to be quite spectacular after a good rain. It is a very unprepossessing trickle otherwise."

"Had there been rain?"

"No. It was very disappointing."

"Oh?" As disappointing as their conversation was proving with so little of her face to be seen?

"Yes," she went on. "In fact, the entire excursion would have been rather flat had it not been for Giovanni."

An unnamed anger rose within him, an anger he directed at the hat that so completely guarded her expressive features. "And what did he do that proved so very noteworthy?" He could not hide his sarcasm.

She peered at him around the stiff brim. "He walked right up to me, a complete stranger, with the kind of smile that one offers only to those with whom one is acquainted, and told me how thrilled he was to see a familiar face."

"Familiar? Well, you were certainly not wearing this bonnet that day."

"No. How did you know?"

"There is too little of your face to be seen for anyone to deem it familiar."

"You do not like it?"

What a heel he was, to have insulted the bloody bonnet. She was doubtless proud of it and hoping for compliments, not insult. Stopping her so that they stood face-to-face, he forced her to look at him, tilting her face upward with a knuckle beneath her lowered chin. "I would far rather look at your expressive features, Nutmeg, than the most fashionable and flattering of bonnets."

"Oh!" She blushed. Her hand rose, brushed his, bringing her blush to deeper hue as she loosed the rustling ribbon that tied the bonnet in place. "Better?" She lifted it from her head.

"Much better," he agreed, tousling her flattened curls.

"Now do go on with your story. You were telling me Giovanni thought he recognized you?"

"Yes. I assured him we had never met before, that he was mistaken in assuming we had."

"Did he explain himself?"

She dangled the bonnet from its black ribbons, carefully smoothing all wrinkles from the ties that had gone beneath her chin. "He puzzled over it a bit, apologizing all the while and reasserting over and over again that he never forgot a face, and was it not possible we had encountered one another."

"Had you?"

"No. He introduced himself to Gussie and Tom, neither of whom he found in the least familiar, introduced us in turn to Lord Frost and his sister, whom he had met up with in transit from Italy to England. We compared notes on any place in which the two of us might have met."

"Any luck?"

"None." She began to twirl the dangling bonnet, a gesture so childlike it roused Reed's most protective feelings.

"Was it all pretense then? A ploy to get to know you."

She blushed, and letting go the bonnet, allowed the twisted ribbons to unwind in a feather-flying whirl of black and white. "No. He remembered at last. It was a statue I reminded him of."

"Dear God! Not the satyr?"

"Yes, Reed, the satyr. But please do not take the Lord's name in vain on my account." She seemed to realize how unladylike her handling of the bonnet had become. Smoothing the ribbons, she allowed the bonnet to hang lifelessly from her hand, more of a coal scuttle than ever.

"I do apologize," he blurted, "but blast it all, I feel the perfect fool! You might never have met the fellow but for my blunder."

"Strange, isn't it, how life has thrown me, so soon,

into the path of one of those who purchased my likeness in bronze?"

"Strange, indeed." Reed could not like it that Giovanni, of all people, should have possession of Megan, if only in the form of a bronze statue. "Did you ask him if you might buy the thing?"

"I did not! I cannot afford such luxuries. I merely agreed that it was a strange coincidence and let the matter drop."

She was accustomed to practicing economies.

"Wisest, I suppose," he said. Considering the uncertain state of his own finances, he had best get used to practicing economies as well.

They had reached the lake. Reed stood looking at the still, shadowed surface, listening to the occasional plop of a trout breaking the surface in search of insects, accompanied by the descending scale song of a warbler and the distant, explosive call of a coot. A heron stalked away from them—long-necked elegance in the shallows. A frog began to sing a ratchety tune.

She sighed. "Giovanni insists it is Fate, or Destiny, or some such nonsense brings us together."

"What kind of fellow is he? Do you care for him?"

A moorhen paddled past, red-faced head pumping. Her wake was all that remained evident of the bird's passage by the time Megan gave answer.

"I do like him. He is creative, a good listener, and generous. As to what kind of fellow he may be, Frost tells me that his father raises prize horses and bottles a remarkable wine, that he has several enormously productive vineyards outside Palermo. He would appear to have no shortage of money. It was he who treated us to the entertainments we enjoyed the night you arrived."

He bent to pick up a stone and skipped it hard across the lake, wishing he might fling Giovanni so far.

"And the Frosts?"

"What of them?"

"What do you know of them?"

"Very little, although I have had the impression on more than one occasion that they preferred having Giovanni to themselves. What do you think of them?" Her smile faded. She bit down on her lower lip. "Laura Frost would seem to be quite taken with you."

He skipped another stone, resolving in that instant to post a letter to his father in London inquiring into the backgrounds of both Giovanni Giamarco and the Frosts. He might be strapped for cash, but he still had connections.

"I hope you don't mind me saying, but I wouldn't want you getting in over your head, Nutmeg. This Italian looks the type to dally with a girl's affections."

She lifted the bonnet like a veil, and placed it once more upon her head. Chin lifted, she formed a jaunty bow. "I am in a mood for dalliance. I mean to educate myself in the art. If anyone is out of their depth it is you."

"Why do you say that?" he asked irritably.

She turned to face the lake, her features shielded from his scrutiny. "I think you are in danger of falling under Laura Frost's spell."

"And if I was, what harm?"

"None, as long as you realize she is cut from the same cloth as Giovanni."

"Why do you think so?"

"Why?" Wry laughter shook the ostrich feathers along the brim of the hat. "Because she is an expert in the art of seduction, Reed. I have watched her mesmerize any male with whom she comes into contact with that high-nosed primness at which she so skillfully pretends. She would eat your heart for breakfast and then get up and leave your empty shell behind her without the least sign of indigestion."

"You are too severe."

The bonnet whirled in his direction. Megan's face was flushed. "Am I? Do you deny then, that she drew you away to work her wiles on you?"

He was shocked by her awareness. "You begin to sound motherly, Megan." He spoke defensively, regretting the words as soon as they were uttered.

She turned away, but not before he saw her wounded expression. "Heaven forbid I should fear for your heart as much as you would seem prepared to fear for mine." Her voice was muffled and sad.

"I am sorry, Nutmeg. Let us not quarrel. I did not come here to quarrel with you."

She did not turn to look at him again, merely stared at the lake and asked hollowly, "Why did you come?"

Chapter Ten

He never did get a chance to tell her. Perhaps that was best.

Augusta and Tom joined them. There was no opportunity for intimate confidences. The four of them walked back to the cottage, where they entertained themselves playing cards until Reed wished the others good night. He went to his room to write his father, asking him for any information he might forward with regard to an Italian by the name of Giovanni Giamarco and his companions Lord and Laura Frost. He ended his letter with a list of questions that had to do with his tally of figures and requested an answer with all possible speed. His fears grew daily upon examination of the ledgers.

It occurred to Reed, that it was wisest, after all, to hold tongue on all that he had meant to disclose to Megan. His financial problem was, after all, family business.

That thought manifested itself again to him on the following day. The manifestation was a man, and the man but a dark speck on the hillside emerging from the larger darkness that was the Buttermere Green Slate Quarry on Honister Crag.

"Look there! A trail barrow." Tom pointed out the moving figure to the party of seven who had gathered for a sight-seeing excursion of the quarry. He had to shout to be heard above the constant ring of chisels hammered against stone. They stood watching from the finishing floor, a raw, leveled area at the base of the hill where it had been demonstrated that the huge chunks of gray-green slate were hammered into slabs along the grain. Reed's artistic sensibilities were more absorbed by the play of light and shadow across the beautiful, muted green shards of slate than by the men who worked them.

"These slabs," Tom, who knew about such things, explained, "are broken into 'clogs' which men called 'rivers'"—he pointed out the appropriate workers—"split into individual slates and hand over to 'dressers' who chisel away the edges, finishing the job."

"The trail barrow he mentioned. Does he mean that dark speck up there?" Laura Frost spoke coyly into Reed's ear. "May I look at him through one of those curious lenses you carry?"

"They will do you no good . . ." He started to explain that the image would be made smaller, not magnified as she doubtless wanted. She did not, or would not, hear him.

"Please." Her breath tickled humidly. "Pretty please."

Rather than shout his excuses to her, or use her ear as she used his, he handed her the folio of Claude glasses. Observing them, Megan arched her brows in a suggestive manner, as if she caught him in the middle of an illicit exchange. How much higher would her brows have risen had she been privy to yesterday's exchanges?

"Useless!" Miss Frost distracted him with another hiss, her hand possessively upon his shoulder as she returned the Claude glasses. "These do not enlarge upon the subject at all."

Reed looked Megan's way again, concerned she might misinterpret Miss Frost's attentions. But Megan was watching the slater on the hillside while Tom waved at them to follow him away from the worst of the noise.

"He pulls a sledge that has been loaded with slate along a track up there, by way of two handles," he shouted. "Like a horse, he goes before it. Can you see the thing kicking up dust behind him?"

Reed could. Miss Frost made no effort to look. She

leaned heavily on his arm. "What a dreadfully noisy, boring, dirty place this is," she said petulantly. "Take me away from this nasty place, Reed. Please, take me away."

"Away? But we have only just begun to view the place, and I find it fascinating."

He was not the only one. Megan's attention was firmly focused on the barrow man. Pointing to a line that came straight down the mountainside, she shouted above the din. "He does not mean to come down by way of that track, does he?"

"He does," Tom contradicted her.

Even as he spoke the man plunged over the edge, the dark shape of his barrow fast on his heels.

"Oh dear," shrieked Gussie. "Has he lost control of the thing?"

"No," Megan gasped. "But it is sheer madness, what he is doing."

Indeed, Reed was rather shocked by the spectacle himself. Did the man mean to outrun the heavy barrow straight down the mountainside? It was a reckless endeavor. A single misstep, or a jolt strong enough to wrench his hands from the barrow's stangs and he would be flattened.

"Extremely dangerous," Tom shouted gleefully. "But fascinating to watch. Countless cartloads of sightseers drive down from Borrowdale to watch these fellows make their daily runs."

"Silly fellow!" Miss Frost clutched at Reed's arm. "There are far more sensible ways to make a living, surely."

So distant were they, so noisy their surroundings, that there was no discernible sound connected to the strange progress of the figure in miniature. The sledge gathered speed. The man's racing feet were lifted from the ground. Suspended by his grip upon the barrow's stangs, he rode the incredible force of gravity downward.

"Dear Lord. He'll be killed!" Gussie hid her eyes behind her hand.

She could not stop watching for long. The sledge was a terribly compelling, crashing, grating momentum. Ungoverned and unstoppable, it threatened to engulf them all. Every muscle in the man's highly developed arms and neck bulged in his effort to stay aboard the erratically pitching barrow. Like Hephaestus who had fallen for a day when thrown from Olympus by Zeus, this man seemingly fell down the mountainside for a nerve-wracking stretch of time.

Swept up in the sound, unable to wrench his eyes away, Reed saw in the spectacle a mirrored manifestation of his own struggle. Thrown from his home at an early age, he was an Hephaestus of sorts himself. Like this man, too, his family dragged a heavy load—of debt. It ran along the narrow track of people's goodwill and patience in receiving payments due. A single misstep at this point and the Talcotts would be crushed beneath the momentum of their folly.

In a cascade of dirt and pebbles, the barrow ground to a halt at the dressing ground.

Reed approached the gasping, sweat-drenched, red-faced creature, his pulse as elevated as if he had run the course alongside the man.

"Have you no fear, man?" he asked.

Breathlessly came the answer, "Aye, but I don't let it run away wit' me."

"How heavy is the load?"

"Not so heavy I cannot slide with it down the mountain." The man laughed at his own obscurity. Beneath the grime he looked to be a young fellow.

Reed had to smile, so carefree was the slater's manner, so cavalier his attitude. He thrust out his hand. "I am Reed, Reed Talcott, and it's not every day I have the privilege of shaking the hand of a man who displays such courage."

The slater hesitated to shake Reed's immaculately

gloved hand. "Beggin' your pardon, guv, but I would not ruin your gloves. We use rosin, don't you see, to help in gripping the stangs, and a right nasty mess they would make of your dabblers." He held both hands out, palms up to show the sticky amber smears that grimed his palms. When Reed removed his gloves and thrust forth instead his bare hand, the slater shook his head with a grin, spit on each palm and wiped them as clean as he could down the legs of begrimed corduroy trews before jovially clasping Reed's hand in a grip that threatened to break its every bone.

Reed tried not to wince. How callused and leathery the man's fingers were! He felt as pale and soft and spineless as an earthworm in this weather-worn grip. How would he hold up if required to labor daily? He had done nothing in his life so physically and mentally challenging as was this man's daily run down the mountainside. Withall, the slater seemed happy with his lot. He grinned, brazenly exhibiting a mouthful of uneven, tobacco-stained teeth.

"I reckon that was no more than a quarter ton o' Tom from up top and three more loads I'll be after before the sun goes down," he offered. "Name's Hamish. Care to have a look about? It's no more than half an hour's walk." He pointed to a zigzagging trail that led up the hill.

"Half an hour?" Like a diamond glittering among the shards of slate, Miss Frost drew the attention of most of the workers when she spoke.

"Aye." Hamish grinned outrageously at her. "I can bring you down a mite faster if you don't mind a bumpy ride."

An almost imperceptible hush fell in the steady hammering, as if for the breath of an instant, each and every one of the quarrymen suspended their noise in anticipation of her response to the undeniably outrageous suggestion.

Miss Frost was not at all amused. Nose in the air, she

ignored Hamish, saying tartly to Reed, who was hard put to suspend his amusement at the idea, "Surely we do not need to spend half an hour trudging up the side of a mountain to look at what amounts to nothing more than a hole in the ground?" She did not speak unduly loud, but her words, beautifully enunciated, carried.

Reed watched the light of interest fade in the eyes of a courageous man, and felt shame that a lady should be so heartless in expressing herself. With a polite tug on his forelock, Hamish hoisted an empty barrow upon his shoulders, as if it were a shell, and set off up the mountain, turtlelike.

"Penny for your thoughts." Oblivious to her own impact, Miss Frost attempted to charm Reed with the same tongue that had just cut into his fellow man.

"I was thinking, that there, but for the grace of God, go I." He said the words softly, and yet they carried. Megan turned to look at him with an expression of approval.

Miss Frost laughed.

Giovanni, who had been silent up to this point, spread his arms in a grand gesture and turned his sorrowful gaze upon the group. "Let us go. It pains me to see such a scar upon the land."

A week earlier, Reed would have agreed with Giovanni. The maps with which he papered his walls were dedicated to a depiction of the mark man made upon pristine British soil. Yet in watching Hamish trudge away from them, Reed realized his outlook had been too simplistic, too removed from the realities these men faced every day in making a living.

Tom responded to Giovanni's remark with a chuckle. "It was your invading countrymen, the Romans, who first started these quarries, Giovanni. They were clever enough to realize that slate made a superior roofing material for their granaries."

Giovanni flung back his head and ran his fingers through the artistic marvel that was his hair. "I apologize for my countrymen They have blemished the face of England."

Megan was regarding the Italian intently—too intently for Reed's taste. "Is this quarry a blemish, then?" she asked. "Or is it instead a monument to man? See you no evidence of imagination, of ingenuity here?' Even courage. I do."

Reed was impressed by the sensible nature of her question. Not so, Giovanni.

"You cannot truly believe such blasphemy."

Megan's chin rose. "Why not? This is a scene that brings to my mind the story of David and Goliath—tiny men chipping away at a mountain's knees, courageously wrestling a living out of nothing more than stone."

"I agree with Giovanni," Miss Frost declared. "There is nothing in the least picturesque in this business."

"The picturesque is a pursuit of the leisure class," Megan snapped. "The penny-wise and pound foolish throw away their riches on such folly, hiring hermits to live in huts, building imitation ruins and grottos in their gardens—all undeniably picturesque and yet I find something grotesque in such wasteful ways being deemed acceptable while men who toil to feed and clothe their families are condemned. Would you put Hamish out of work, Miss Frost, in the name of the picturesque? Would you pauper any of these hardworking fellows?" She waved a hand.

Laura eyed her with undisguised contempt and pretended she was confused. "Do you know I cannot hear more than one word in four above this din, Miss Breech. Do you mind repeating yourself, or was it after all, of no importance?"

No one else seemed to have remained deaf to Megan's words.

Giovanni was frowning, dark eyebrows knit above troubled eyes. "Nature is violated that men might fill their stomachs?" he suggested.

Megan nodded. "Why would God have created so varied and plentiful a world if He did not expect men to make use of it?"

"Change stimulates growth," Tom took up the argument. "And growth stimulates progress."

Giovanni flung up his hands. "Growth! Bah! A plague on progress. The mountain does not grown. It is, in fact, diminished before our very eyes. What price prosperity? Do we pay homage to the mountain in raiding her of her riches or is this, instead, a rape in our passion for growth?"

"Change is not all bad." Tom cheerfully tried to diffuse the growing tension. "Only look at what is being done to the center of London. Streets widened, nasty tenements torn down. Where vermin once troubled the heart of the city, beautiful new rows of houses stand. It is inevitable that man will leave his mark on even the most remote of areas."

"Well, Reed"—Megan prodded him—"what have you to add?"

"Me?" Reed shrugged. "I think that no matter how much we might wish things would remain the same, change is inevitable, a vehicle either for growth or for destruction. It is up to the individual to determine in which direction it takes him."

The direction Reed's curiosity took him was up the mountainside. He felt himself a Pied Piper of sorts. Megan fell in beside him, then Frost, Gussie, and Tom. In the end, only Giovanni and Miss Frost refused to make the climb. In a way, Reed was relieved. The Italian was an uncomfortable reminder to him that he could no longer expect to monopolize Megan's time and attention, and Miss Frost annoyed him, always hanging on his arm and breathing hotly into his ear.

The quarry was unusual, well worth the effort it took to hike to the mouth of its man-made cavern. Unlike most of the quarries in the district, it was not open to the weather. Strange, too, was the sight of men with tallow candle stubs attached to the brims of their caps dangling from chains in the ceilings as they brought the slate down from above as well as below.

"A bit like a cathedral, this," Gussie said as they craned their necks to stare at the arched ceilings.

A slab of slate crashed to the floor of the cavern. Rock splinters flew. Both women flinched.

Megan eyed the heights. "I would guess that so real is the potential of sudden death that one cannot help but be reminded of one's maker here."

Reed decided the place was not so much a cathedral as it was an abbey for the men, who slept in makeshift shanties at the quarry site, going home to their loved ones no more often than on the weekends. It seemed a hard life. Lonely, too. The most interesting aspect of the quarry was its birds. Carrier pigeons were used to wing speedy messages over the mountains, not only to the quarry's main offices, but also to wives and families.

To whom would he send messages, Reed wondered as they walked back down the zigzag path to their horses. His mother, his father, and Megan came to mind. No one else. Who else cared for him? Who else did he care for? And Megan might soon be marrying.

"Do you mean to invest in a quarry, then?"

It was Frost who asked. The question pulled Reed from the well of his thoughts. Invest in a slate quarry? The idea was an intriguing one.

He shrugged. "Can't say. As it stands I haven't the ready to do anything of the kind."

"Oh? I could see no other reason for the intensity of your interest." Frost drew forth a silver case from which he extracted a cigar. "Have you money troubles?" He offered the case to Reed, who shrugged it and the question aside. Surely his financial status was too personal a matter to discuss with a gentleman he ill knew. He had been loose-tongued to let slip as much as he had.

"Never seems to be enough of the stuff hanging about, does there?" Frost made light of the question as he lipped the cigar and tucked the case back into his pocket. His expression serious, he slowed his pace so that they fell behind the others, all the while patting his pockets until he found what he was looking for, a silver cigar cutter. He pulled the cigar from between his lips. "I've a question to ask of a rather personal nature. I hope you don't mind."

More personal than the condition of his finances? Reed was intrigued. He frowned. "Yes?"

"Miss Megan Breech?"

What about Megan. "Yes?"

"Are you in love with her?" Frost asked the question as bluntly as he snipped the end of the cigar.

"What?" Reed had heard plain enough. He reacted to the frank question as he had reacted to the man's sister the day before, with a sense of disbelief. "What you ask is personal indeed. Why do you wish to know?"

Frost spread his hands, as if to smooth the air between them, the cigar like a bent and discolored sixth finger. "Laura says you must be in love."

"What led her to believe that?"

"She told me she has gone out of her way to flirt with you. That you are completely resistant to her charms. They are considerable, you must admit."

"Of course." Reed floundered.

This time it was a silver matchbox that emerged from the man's pockets. "The reason I ask, is that I am myself captivated by the young lady's passion."

"Passion? Your sister's?"

Frost laughed heartily as he struck the match, held it to the end of the cigar, and puffed it to smoking life amidst a sulfurous cloud. "I refer to Miss Breech, of course."

"Oh?" Reed had never considered Megan a particularly passionate creature.

"She held forth with remarkable conviction this morning in favor of the working man, don't you agree?" Frost's lips, Reed noticed as they puckered to blow a series of smoke rings, were thick, rosy, and as damp as the end of the cigar he pulled from his mouth whenever he spoke. He had never really noticed the man's mouth before. Strange, that it should so fascinate him now.

He nodded, bothered by the smoke blown his way. "Megan has always been excellent at argument," he said. "She is both intelligent and erudite."

"Passionately so," Frost reiterated, licking at his already wet lips.

Passionate? The word, and the way it was uttered, struck Reed as inappropriate. His dear, sweet, naive Megan, was she a passionate creature?

Frost troubled him further in admitting, with a suggestive chuckle that belched breathy little smoke clouds, "I should like to redirect some of that passion—but would not care to step on toes if you two are in some way committed to one another."

Reed did not care for such ill-bred suggestiveness. "We are committed to one another by eleven years of friendship. I would not encourage you to trifle with her affections in any way, nor would I think you shall be offered much opportunity with Giovanni so firmly planted between the two of you."

Frost laughed from behind a veritable cloud bank and flicked ash from his cigar. "Giovanni is captivated by all things female. Females are in turn captivated by the depth of his awareness and his appreciation for their gender in general. But he is an inconstant creature."

"You know this, and yet would leave your sister alone in his care?"

Frost chuckled. "Laura can take care of herself."

Yet, when they reached the bottom of the hill, it appeared Frost overestimated his sister's self-sufficiency. Laura Frost had been swept completely off her feet by the Italian. She was resting, and quite comfortably it would appear, in Giovanni Giamarco's cradling arms.

Chapter Eleven

The more she was around Laura Frost, the less Megan cared for her. The young woman reminded her of a vine. It did not seem to matter that it was always a different fellow, only that there should be *someone* male to wind herself around.

"My ankle has been twisted on one of these dreadful rocks," she said primly from the harbor of Giovanni's arms. "Terribly tedious, I know, but Giovanni has offered to ride back with me, to Grasmere, while the rest of you continue your explorations."

"Unless your brother insists on accompanying you."

Giovanni looked to Frost, who waved away the idea, saying, "Good of you to go with her."

Augusta and Tom were all sympathy.

"How dreadful for you," Gussie crooned.

Tom questioned the propriety of the proposed plan. "Surely you will not want to go back with only Mr. Giamarco for company?"

Gussie agreed. "Perhaps we should curtail our side trip to the Falls and make our way back to Grasmere with you."

Megan thought her sister completely taken in by Miss Frost's wiles.

Miss Frost did not sound at all inclined to lead a cavalcade back to Grasmere. In fact, she seemed to protest too much. "It was not my intention to divert the rest of you from the day's entertainments. It will be a tedious journey. We mean to go very slowly, so as not to jolt my poor foot unnecessarily."

Neither Tom nor Gussie voiced any objection to Megan continuing on to view the Jaws of Borrowdale and Lodore Falls, as long as Reed saw to her safety. The two groups of riders parted company at the village of Longthwaite.

Megan's threesome, for Lord Frost came with them, set briskly off along a road that paralleled the Borrowdale River, north to the village of Grange. The afternoon was perfect for their excursion. The sky held no more than a wisp of cloud. The breeze was fresh with the smell of clover, heather, and fern. The race of the river and the rustling voices of oak, beech, and alder were the only sounds to be heard, apart from the noises their horses made and the occasional alarm of a startled bird.

Just south of Grange, on the birch-covered slopes of Grange Fell, they stopped to examine what was known as the Bowder Stone, an enormous cube-shaped boulder, delicately poised on one edge and as tall as a town house.

It was in examining the oddity that Megan noticed how little Reed had to say, while Frost went to the opposite extreme and could not be stopped from expounding at length on his detailed theories as to how and why such an enormous boulder came to sit so precariously on a well-treed hillside.

When they rode on, the steeply wooded fellsides closing in on the boulder-strewn track the closer they got to Derwentwater Lake, Lord Frost seemed bent on closing in on her as well, while Reed, if anything, became more distant. In brooding silence, he followed their amiable, chattering progress through a thickly wooded gorge, behind which rose the wild, grand hills referred to as the Jaws of Borrowdale.

It was a beautiful prospect, a sight worth seeing, as was Lodore Falls, though it had not been fed recently by rain, and the water's flow was considerably diminished.

Throughout their progress, Reed remained strangely quiet and distracted, allowing Megan's attention and conversation to be monopolized by Lord Frost, whose companionship she tolerated more than enjoyed. Why had Reed come so far if he meant to be melancholy? Perhaps this was tame stuff to one so newly returned from a jaunt through the wonders of the Continent. Far more lowering, she must seem fairly tame stuff compared to Laura Frost. Perhaps Reed wished himself on the road to Grasmere.

In the end, it was a mundane encounter with three axemen that got Reed to talking. The axemen were loading two wagons with the long, stripped poles they had cut from the stunted oak boles of a coppice wood.

"Where is the wood bound?" he asked.

One of the men cheerfully explained that the first wagon was bound for a local bobbin mill, while the second was to be fired into charcoal by local colliers. Reed went on to ask several other questions, the gist of which was unintelligible to Megan because Frost, who was not in the least interested in the wood, other than to complain that the bristling wagons blocked their way, assumed she, too, could not be interested in the exchange. Rudely, he regaled Megan with a long-winded account of his appreciation of her fine seat horseback. In addition, he expounded at length on his own prowess at sitting a horse when it came to jumping walls and fences in the hunt.

"I do love a good hunt!" He reined his horse off the road and into the stunted oaks in order to pass the wagons. "Do you care to accompany me, Miss Breech, on a fox hunt the locals form tomorrow? It promises to be ripping good sport over challenging ground. Both Giovanni and my dear sister are mad to go."

Megan might have thought Reed paid them no mind had he not chosen to interrupt before she could open her mouth.

"I would remind you, Megan, that you have promised to go boating with me tomorrow."

She turned in the saddle, mouth ajar. She had promised him nothing of the kind.

He winked at her.

"Another time, perhaps," said Frost.

"Perhaps," she said, fervently hoping another time would not present itself. She did not like concocting falsehoods any more than she liked to make sport of chasing down and killing animals. She made a point of reining her mount in beside Reed's.

He seemed to welcome the opportunity to share a word with her. "Do you know I have always found the process by which coppicing is done to be rather repugnant?"

"There is something grotesque in the deformed stunting of so much potential," she agreed.

He nodded. "Yes. I always saw that much of it. The negative. Nothing more. Today, I cannot help thinking that in these mangled limbs there is a positive to be seen."

"A positive?"

"Yes. A beauty and hope, in the very persistence of these trees to continue to put forth growth despite having been cut off at the knees."

Megan gave him a searching look. "You surprise me!"

"Do I?"

He smiled and though she steeled herself against it, his smile left her feeling like toffee inside, all sweet and soft and gooey.

"I am pleased to hear I can still surprise you, Nutmeg. As many years as we have known one another I might have thought everything about me so well known as to have become completely predictable."

She studied him thoughtfully. "Am I predictable?"

He looked surprised she should ask. "No, Megan," he said very softly, "I rediscover you every day."

With the cool, moist darkness of evening at their heels, the trio returned to Grasmere. The homey odors of cooked turnips, roasting fish, and toasted cheese accosted them as they passed through the village. Reed was the first to dismount in the empty stableyard of the inn where they had rented their hacks.

"I shall just go in and settle our accounts," he offered.

"By all means." Frost interrupted another of his self-absorbed diatribes to nod agreeably.

Megan said nothing, but Reed heard her laugh at some witticism with which Frost enthralled her. The man was annoying, so great was the gift of his conversation. Reed turned as he reached the doorway to the inn.

Frost was helping Megan from her horse. A simple thing, really, but so familiar was their pose, it startled Reed. Megan had loosed her boot from the stirrup, unhooked her knee from the horn of the sidesaddle, and placed her hands on Frost's shoulders. He reached up to grab her by the waist, swung her down from the horse's back, turning with enough vigor to send her skirts whirling about his torso. For the fraction of an instant all the lines and planes lined up like the pieces of a puzzle, perfectly fitted. There, in front of Reed's eyes were the lovers—his bronze lovers, come to life.

It crossed his mind that Megan might find Lord Frost attractive—that she saw in him the potential for passion. The idea angered and disappointed him in a way he could not remember feeling angry or disappointed in a long time.

"Do you care for Frost?" he asked Megan later when Frost had parted with them at the top of the lane.

"He's nice enough," she said noncommittally.

Nice enough for what? Reed wondered.

"He is a prodigious conversationalist." She laughed.

"As are you," he said.

"Am I?"

"Mmm-hmm." He nodded. The only difference being

he never tired of her conversation, whereas Lord Frost
was a bloody great bore.

"How lovely it is here," she whispered. "With nothing
but the rustle of the wind in the trees and the distant hoot
of an owl."

He enjoyed the quiet for a moment before he murmured, "A blessed thing, silence."

"Especially when one's ears have been jangling all
day with unwanted noise."

She meant Lord Frost. He smiled.

"You have been very quiet today," she said softly.

"Have I?"

"No more than a dozen words have passed your lips."

He shrugged. "I am not a prodigious conversationalist."

She smiled. He knew she smiled from the sound of
her voice, though the light was too poor to see much of
her expression. "Gabby you have never been," she
agreed.

"There *is* something I would like to talk to you
about," he said hesitantly.

"Mmm? What?" She stifled a yawn and slipped her
hand into the crook of his arm.

It occurred to him that what he had to say was best
discussed when she was fresh. "Tomorrow," he said
softly, patting her hand. "It can wait until tomorrow.
Tonight, I prefer to enjoy the silence with you."

Chapter Twelve

Reed lowered his Claude glass to relieve the ache in his arms. The watercolor he was painting was almost done. It did not perfectly mimic the landscape to be seen from the bank of Grasmere Lake, but that was entirely intended. His works were usually romantically embellished, according to the artistic license of Claude and Rosa. In this case, the mountains had been slightly rearranged, one hilltop made more rugged, another removed altogether. A clump of trees had been moved from the right side of the middle ground of reality to the left foreground. Several figures, in addition to Gussie and Tom, had been added as points of interest, afloat and fishing. It was a fine, picturesque bit of work. Not the best Reed had ever done, and yet certainly not the worst. Strangely, he found himself dissatisfied—the work unfulfilling. What business had he moving mountains?

If he blinked, he saw in his mind's eye rows of numbers that did not add up, taunting him. He tried not to blink. Instead, he feasted his gaze on the sumptuous banquet of beauty spread before him. As if the picturesque were a soporific, he found himself becalmed, his thoughts and movements languid, even peaceful. All worries for the moment subsided—lost—or if not lost, made very small in the breathtaking sweep of a cerulean sky into which hillside after hillside folded itself, and all of it echoed perfectly in the still mirror of the lake.

For a moment, everything in life and death made

sense. There was a pattern to be seen in nature, a grand scheme—the hand of God.

And yet, he sighed and raised his glass again, he could not find the grand scheme in his current situation. He could not rearrange his life as easily as he rearranged the mountains. Where was the pattern in the loss of all that had been certain and secure in his life? Could it be there was none to be seen, no pattern—just chaos?

A splash from the lake and a gleeful "Aha!" from Tom as he assisted Gussie in reeling in a fish.

Megan looked up from her painting to smile at him. "I am so glad you arranged for us to boat down to this end of the lake today," she said. "The view is unsurpassed. The reflections from this spot, on such a clear day, are absolutely remarkable."

"Yes," he agreed. Still looking at the lake, he stood up from his collapsible three-legged stool to stretch his limbs. "Everything perfectly doubled," he murmured.

"Except that *they* are upside down." She pointed at their reflection in the water. "And *we* are right side up. Or is it the other way around? Perhaps we are the ones turned on our heads."

Reed turned his back on the lake and bent to search the grass for skimming stones. With childlike whimsy he looked back through his legs, upside down, at the reflections in the lake.

"What are you doing? Giving my sister a grand view of your better half?" she asked.

He laughed. "What would you do, Nutmeg, if you discovered that everything you had believed to be the truth, everything you had counted on, was turned upside down?" He threw a stone between his legs into the lake, sending ripples through the mirrored image of what appeared to be his sky.

"What would I do?" She took stance beside him, spread-legged and bent over. "I would wait for my head to stop spinning, take stock of my new surroundings . . ."

He heard her bunch the rustling fabric of her skirt,

stole a look at her, and realized she meant to look at the lake the same way he did.

"Then I would get on with life with a whole new outlook. How would you respond?"

She was amazing, his Megan. How many young ladies would so blithely risk their pride by standing as she now stood, her face flushed, her hair falling loose from its pins, her ankles exposed for all the world to see and admire? Rather eye-catching ankles they were, too, clad as they were in chalk-white ribbed stockings. She shot him an amused look, noticed the direction of his gaze, and said, "French! Do you care for them?" She seemed beautiful to him in the intimacy of their ludicrous pose, as she had never seemed beautiful to him before.

"Panic," he blurted, and then he forced himself to laugh, to make his answer less important. "I think I would be panic-struck in dizzy disbelief for a while."

She twisted her head to look at him more closely, her expression rather more serious than it had been. "Has your world been turned upside down in some way, Reed?"

"Let's assume that it has. Otherwise, the blood would not be rushing to my head the way it is."

She laughed, as he had intended she should. "Well, generally the answers to our troubles are right in front of our noses if we will only look for them. I would ask you, what do you long for most?"

"Long for?" She was eyeing him keenly, at least he thought she was, it was rather difficult to ascertain with her eyes upside down as they were, and her cheeks sagging the wrong way. "I do not follow."

"Well, it is a matter of priorities, you see. If everything has been turned upside down it would be of highest priority to determine what in your life is most important to set straight. Then, it would be simpler to decide just what you could adapt to in its altered state. The changed perspective might even be a blessing."

A shout from the lake—Tom demanding, "What arsey-varsey is this then?"

Megan dropped her skirt back into decorum and shot up and around to shout back, "We are engaged in a lesson on perspective."

"Is that right?" Tom's laughter bounced over the water.

Reed, too, stood and turned.

Gussie was laughing. "From our perspective, Megan, your lesson is neither proper nor ladylike."

Reed murmured. "It all depends on one's perspective, doesn't it?"

Quick and keen Megan looked at him. "Is it money woes?"

He felt as transparent as his Claude glass beneath her steady gaze. "Why do you ask?"

"Oh, come now. You have had your nose buried in ledgers full of figures since you arrived." She reached out to touch his forehead. "And there is a line here, where I have never noticed one before. It will not go away, even when you laugh."

He drew back from her touch and turned to stare at the reflection of the mountain, the whispered memory of her finger against the flesh of his forehead. "We all have problems," he said elusively, unwilling to lay another mountain at her feet. "I am happy today to be in your company. I wonder if you would mind me keeping you from your friends for one more day before I leave."

"Leave? You mean to go? So soon?"

"Yes." He frowned. "I do but wait for correspondence from my father. What he has to say will determine whether I go home first, or straight to London."

"London? Will you be in London when I arrive there?"

He shrugged. "I cannot say. I have business that may take me there."

She seemed content with his answer. "Perhaps we can visit the National Gallery together."

"Perhaps," he said doubtfully. Viewing collections of paintings was not going to be the first order of business should he end up in London.

Megan took guilty pleasure in the news that she might see more of Reed in London. Guilty because, as she reminded herself, she must not hold on to false hope.

That evening, when Giovanni and the Frosts dropped in at the cottage to see if anyone cared to go for a stroll in the gathering gloom, her hopes were threatened by an event most unexpected. It began when they divided up, and in her estimation the division was a highly unsatisfactory affair.

Tom interested Lord Frost in a nip of brandy and the smoking of a cigar. The two of them declined to walk at all. Giovanni gallantly took Megan on one arm and her sister on the other. This put Miss Frost momentarily out of sorts until, with a toothsome smile, she leaned—too heavily, Megan thought—on Reed's arm, all the while complaining that her ankle was not yet feeling altogether better and did he mind going very slowly for her sake.

Ever the gentleman, Reed slowed his progress to a snail's pace. Megan's energetic, chattering threesome soon left the pair behind. Giovanni did his best to charm both of the women he escorted. He was, Megan decided, as pleasant as the balmy breeze that cooled their brows, as pleasant as the soft cooing of a dove, as pleasant as pleasant could be. And yet, she could not stop thinking of Reed and Miss Frost and what they might be saying, or doing together, in the growing darkness.

What they had found to do she saw all too publicly displayed in the moonlit walk back to the cottage. Unexpectedly, their trio came upon the pair as they rounded a curve in the shrubbery-screened track. Before them unfolded a scene Megan would never have believed had she not witnessed it.

Limned by moonlight, Reed held Miss Frost uplifted

in his arms, her feet quite removed from all contact with the ground. In this posture they were kissing! Kissing!

Megan was pained and shocked by the sight! Reed, she thought, had but to grow hair on his haunches and horns from his head and he was a bronzed satyr with an unwilling woman in his arms. The all-too passionate exchange was made all the more shocking by the fact that Miss Frost was beating Reed's upper arms with the flats of both hands. He released her abruptly, with a choked, even a pained sound, looking shocked and bewildered, his mouth covered by his hand.

Miss Frost, on the other hand, let loose a screech that sent roosting birds winging. "How dare you!" she cried. "You monster! How dare you take advantage of me in such an improper fashion?"

"How thare I? You bip me! I'm rudthy well bleething." This unintelligible exclamation erupted from behind the hand Reed held to his mouth.

"Oh my!" Gussie gasped.

Miss Frost turned a tear-stained face in their direction. "Giovanni!" she wailed. "Thank heaven you have come." She ran to him, flinging herself into his comforting arms, where she wept against his shirtfront in a most affecting manner.

"What is this!" Giovanni fairly exploded. "What have you done to her, you scoundrel?"

"Me?" Reed sounded plaintiff. The explanation that followed was no more coherent than before. "I haff done nuthang. She bip ma tang!" He moved his hand away from his mouth. Both were red with blood.

"Dear God. Has he gone mad? What is he saying?" Gussie said.

"I believe he is saying that Miss Frost bit his tongue," Megan hazarded.

Reed nodded enthusiastically. "Yeth. Yeth. Ow!"

"Though why she should have access to his tongue in the first place is beyond me."

"Indeed!" Gussie huffed. "I am shocked and appalled. There can be no excuse for such behavior."

"No excuses," Giovanni strongly agreed. "Only apologies." He glared pointedly at Reed.

"Apologithze?" Reed looked at him incredulously as he dabbed at his tongue with his handkerchief. "Affer thith?" He pointed at his mouth.

"You will apologize at once or I shall expect satisfaction of you!" Giovanni insisted.

"Ha!" Eyes blazing, Reed approached Miss Frost, who cowered, whimpering, in Giovanni's arms.

"You stay away from me," she cried out. "I thought you were a gentleman."

"And I, mathame"—he bowed—"having mithtaken you for a lady, mothe humbly beg your pardon. Intheed, I exthtend thinthere regreths that our paths ever crothed. Ith there any way I can atone for my folly in having been tho completely taken in by you?"

When he received no response, Reed turned on his heel. Still daubing his handkerchief to his tongue, he stalked away. He left the others absolutely speechless. Even Miss Frost ceased her whimpering.

Giovanni's face flushed crimson. "You are a complete cad, sir," he called after Reed's retreating figure.

Reed's answer floated back to them from the darkness. "You, thir, are the complethe fool."

Angry, hurt, and betrayed, Megan caught up with Reed outside the cottage. He seemed to wait for her in the darkness. He had sat himself down just opposite the cottage door, on a stile that bridged the stone wall edging the lane. "And do you, too, believe I mend to harm Mith Frotht?" he asked softly.

"Is there good reason why I should not believe what I saw plainly with my own eyes, Reed? Really! How could you?"

"Id wath nod as id appeared," he protested vehemently.

"Oh no? Why don't you tell me what happened then?" Her voice sounded far calmer than she felt. It held only a trace of sarcasm. Never had her trust in Reed's intentions been so thoroughly shaken.

"She trigged me," he said angrily, "stho it would look egthactly as it muth have looked to you. I am thtill puthzling out why."

He fell silent. She let the stillness close in around them, unsure of what he might reveal to her—unsure she would be able to bear it if he had really forced himself on an unwilling woman, even Laura Frost, whom she had begun to detest.

"We were walking thlowly along the lane," he said. "I had in fact, thuggested we turn back, tho dependant had Mith Frothst become on my arm for thupport. Her ankle wath troubling her. We heard your approach, the three of you, laughing and talking. All of a thudden, Mith Frost wath not bethide me."

"No?"

"No. She had let go of my arm and wath climbing a thtile."

"A stile? But how could she climb a stile with her ankle hurting her as much as she claims?"

He shrugged and shook his head. "I cannot imagine whad pothethed her."

"She climbed the stile. What then?"

He sighed, jumped down from the stile, and turned to look at it, as if imagining Miss Frost again in his mind. "'Help me down,' she called to me." He nodded to an imaginary Miss Frost. He waved a hand at Megan. "Pretend to be her."

Megan hesitated.

"Pleathe."

"You do not expect me to bite your tongue, or kiss you, or anything like that do you?"

He snorted. "No!"

She accepted his assistance in scaling the stile.

"There," he said. "Now, turn and athk me to help you down."

Again she hesitated. "So, you were helping her down? That was what you hope to convince me I saw? Doing it a bit brown, Reed. You were kissing her! Do not try to convince me otherwise."

"Me, kithing her? Farfetched as it may thound, she was kithing me! And not a friendly kith, either. It wath pothitively ravenous! She had my bleething tongue between her teeth to keep me from pulling away, she did!"

"Really Reed," Megan said skeptically. "I am still confused as to how she managed to acquire such an odd grip on you. Get me down from here. I will not believe such a Banbury tale."

He put his hands on either side of her waist, as if to help her down. "But that ith prethithly why I athked you to ged up there. Tho you could thhee."

"Thhee what? I mean, *see* what?"

"In thith position, I cannod compel you to kith me."

He swung her away from the stile, even as he spoke and in demonstration tried to force her to kiss him. For Megan it was very troubling to find herself dependant, if only for an instant, on the strength of his arms, her body leaned into his. Their eyes locked with as much heat as his hands clasped her waist. For a moment all reason abandoned her. She swayed forward, drawn to him in an elemental way over which she seemed to have little control. She wanted him to kiss her. She wanted to know what the warmth of his mouth would feel like against hers. She had every intention of bending her head so that his lips might meet hers, but in making the first move to do just that, her sense of propriety returned. What he had said was true. So high above him was she in position that he could not compel her to kiss him. She would have had to bend over to match her lips to his, just as Miss Frost had bent over, despite the pounding protest of her hands!

"I see!" she whispered, strangely giddy as he lowered her gently to the ground and let go his hold on her.

"You beliefe me?"

Unsteadily, she looked away, unable to face the intensity of expression with which he awaited an answer.

"Pleathe thay you do!" He bent down that he might stare into her eyes—so close he took her breath away. For the second time that day she regretted making such a point of the fact that she had no intention of kissing him.

"Really, Megan. You muth beliefe me. My heart ith broken otherwithe."

She laughed a trifle hysterically at the failings of his tongue. "I believe you," she said quietly, hoping to satisfy him, so that he would pull away. Otherwise she would fall into his arms.

"Thank God!" He stood up straight again with a heartfelt sigh.

Feeling hot and breathless, Megan smoothed her dress, her hands brushing the very spots where Reed had held her as he helped her down. "It is Gussie and Tom who will have trouble swallowing the tale," she warned him.

"Thounds a great faradithel, doeth it?"

"A faradiddle indeed," she agreed.

Chapter Thirteen

It took a great deal of explaining, but in the end, even Tom and Gussie were convinced that Miss Frost had behaved very queerly, and Reed had not after all, divested himself of all decency.

"Cunning young woman," Gussie said as she offered Reed a cold tea-leaf compress for his mouth. "I wonder what she can be after to have used you so shamelessly, and with such careful timing that all of us should see and misinterpret things exactly as she wanted us to."

"The woman is a brazen tease," Tom said.

"I think she did it to regain Giovanni's shtraying intereth," Reed mumbled around the compress.

"She did run straight into his arms," Gussie agreed thoughtfully. "But I do not understand why she should be so keen to have him,"

"I am relieved to hear you say as much, dearest," Tom said jovially, "but I am a little surprised as well. I would have thought Giovanni Giamarco the ideal that every other gentleman must be held up to. He is rich, handsome, and singularly attentive to whatever woman he happens to be with."

"Rich? Isth he?" Reed asked around the edge of the compress, his interest keener than Megan had expected.

"Aye! Rich as Croesus to hear Lord Frost tell the tale. Land, prize horses, acres of vineyards, an incomparable art collection, and more."

Reed frowned. "I had no notion."

Gussie made an expansive gesture with her hands. "I

would not have him if I could. I find him too inconstant in his attentions. No woman can like that in a potential husband."

"Am I constant then," Tom asked, bussing her on the cheek.

"As constant and dependable as the ticking of a clock, my love," she said affectionately.

"But not half so annoying I hope."

She laughed. They all went away to bed laughing, but not until Tom, too, evidenced his completely restored confidence in Reed in saying, "Do you still mean to make the trip to Keswick tomorrow?"

"Have you any objection?" Reed asked.

"No, no. To the contrary. It will be far harder for Giovanni to call you out, or some such foolishness, if we disappear for the day."

Disappear they did, though Megan and Reed did not go to Keswick to shop as Gussie and Tom did. They went instead, armed with sketchbooks, watercolors, and easels, to a hillside a few miles east of the town where the Castlerigg standing stones dominated a slight promitory.

There were clouds blotting the sky, thick, fleecy clouds, like grazing Herdwick sheep above the mountaintops. They promised rain, perhaps on the morrow, which to Megan seemed completely in keeping with Reed's intention to abandon them. The sun had as much difficulty penetrating the white masses as she had in finding reasons to smile. The cloud's underbellies, like her spirits, were thrown into shadow, as were the folds of the mountains and hills that blued the horizon. Was her future, a future without Reed beside her, as shadowed as the landscape?

She hoped not.

As it turned out, it was the perfect day to view the stone circle. There was a quiet mystery to the place, a sense of waiting, a sort of hushed holiness. As they first caught sight of the standing stones, shards of golden sunshine broke through the clouds just above the hilltop. As if the light were God's fingers, it reached down to touch the circle of thirty-odd weathered stones.

"Heaven help us, Nutmeg! Look at it!" Reed exclaimed, flipping out his sketchpad, that his pencil might capture the mystery of light and shadow.

Megan did not immediately busy herself with her own pencils and charcoal. She was possessed of no great desire to paint. Instead, she walked among the stones, staring, touching, losing herself in a sense of awe. The worn dog's teeth circle was more oval than round. When she came to their center she turned slowly, her gaze traveling busily over each of the monumental boulders until she came to the sight of Reed. His attention was focused in intent if flickering bursts, first on the view before him as seen through his umber Claude glass, and then on what his darting pencil portrayed in his sketchbook. She wished he might focus so intently on her.

"What stories they might tell," she said. "Imagine. How they came to be here. What effort it took to gather them together. What purpose they have served."

What purpose did the yearning she suffered for Reed serve? Why did her heart ache with longing for this man, who recognized it not?

"One cannot help but wonder why," he said, his pencil never wavering. "Why did they bother? It had to be a huge bother, don't you agree? Carting these enormous bits of rock here. Setting them up just so. The locals say they are Druid temples of some sort. Worshipping the sun, or some such nonsense."

Megan regarded the stones. Why could she not harden her heart like these stones, that it might better weather the storms of love and desire? "I wonder," she said softly, "is this cursed or blessed ground?"

Was her love, her desire, her longing a curse, or a blessing?

"That is a question better directed at your father. I suppose, as someone once pointed out to me, it is a matter of perspective." He was smiling when she looked back at him, well aware that he threw her own words back in her face.

Thoughtfully, she walked the circle of stones. A matter of perspective. The events of the last few days had shaken her resolve to subdue and forget forever her love for Reed. Was that, too, no more than a matter of perspective? Her feelings made no more sense than this gathering of stones, but there was something admirable in them, if only in their persistence.

As she passed each of the stones, she took advantage of their bulk to blot momentarily from her sight the image of Reed, only to marvel at the manner in which her heart quickened when he popped, quite predictably, into view again on the other side. She studied his face from every angle, the light changing. She committed to memory the tilt of his head, the line of his jaw, the curve of his cheek. She missed him now, before they where even separated. The color of his hair, the flashing brilliance of his smile, the little laugh lines that bordered his eyes and mouth—heavy as stones these things hung in her mind, heavy with her anguish in knowing he meant to leave tomorrow with her love never expressed.

He seemed changed. Or was it only the change in their surroundings and in the company they kept? Another stone to blot him from her sight, another fresh perspective and still she came to the same conclusion. Her oldest and dearest friend, the man she had vowed to detach all thought and feeling from—she was more in love with him than ever.

Time would not change that. It could not wear it away, any more than time and weather had worn away these stones.

All her life, Megan had found comfort and answers in the Bible from which her father spoke to his congregation every Sunday. She sought comfort now, among the many verses she had memorized. As she moved from rock to rock, closer and closer to Reed, she leaned into the hard, sun-warmed surfaces and whispered a prayer from the Psalms. "Have mercy on me O Lord for I am in trouble: mine eye is consumed with grief . . . and my years with sighing."

"Did you say something?" Reed asked.

She pressed her back hard against the largest rock, unwilling to explain. "Father would find the mystery of this place vastly interesting. He would want to know the true history of these stones."

Reed paused in his painting, his expression thoughtful. "True history. Just what do you suppose true history to be?"

"The chronicling of events. What else?"

"I think true history is a difficult thing to collect. I think we do not, any of us, know the true history of any person, place, or thing."

The idea made her uneasy. "Not even when records are kept?"

"No, for the records are kept by an individual. Truth is therefore seen through that person's perspective, just as a painter gives the scene before him his perspective."

"Ah!"

"We have, therefore, one person's interpretation of what true history was and between the lines of that interpretation are truth's secrets."

"Secrets?"

"Yes. Bits unseen and untold. The little mysteries of history. Only think if you had never heard my side of the story last night. You would have quite a different history of the event in your mind this morning."

"I see what you are getting at." Thoughtfully, she unscrewed the cap on the canteen. Splashing water and then pigment on a wide brush she blocked in the light and shadow of Castlerigg Stones without benefit of a starter sketch.

"Are there mysteries in your life of which I know nothing, Nutmeg?" He surprised her with the question.

She laughed, a sad little sound. "Of course there are."

She dipped into pigment again, roughing in the dark, weathered shapes of the standing stones.

It was his turn to be surprised. "Are there big things, Nutmeg? Important things?"

"I perceive them as such."

A peregrine winged above them, slate blue with a black-barred underbelly, powerful and swift. With the flick of her wrist Megan added the bird to the pale wash of her sky.

"You intrigue me," Reed admitted. "I thought you felt free to tell me anything. It pains me to think you guard yourself against me."

"Are there, then, no secrets you keep from me, Reed?"

He opened his mouth, closed it again almost immediately and nodded. "One or two things, come to think of it."

"Mystery can be a good thing, in moderation," she said softly.

"You will not tell me your secrets?"

She eyed the scene before her. Words, thoughts, and feelings pressed hard against the dam of her best intentions, threatening to spill over. How would Reed respond if she were to tell him the true history of her feelings for him? She had thought of little else of late. That secret history hung between them like an unpainted page. She shook her head. "I might, someday, given the right circumstances. And you? Will you tell me why you must rush away tomorrow? And why your forehead grows prematurely wrinkled over the figuring of figures?"

"Someday," he promised. "Someday, I will tell you everything."

The day ended with their secrets still intact and though they had spent the last two days together, Megan felt a growing distance between them. A growing sense of secrets.

Two more had arrived while they were out. Two wax sealed letters had been delivered to the cottage. One came from Reed's father, the other from Giovanni Gia-marco.

Reed tore into both letters. Both made him frown. He did not tell her what news they brought.

She did not ask.

The financial news was not what Reed had hoped for. His father informed him there were no unlisted sources of income, no hidden assets, no hope of sliding out of their financial fiasco easily.

In addition, Lord Talcott could tell him nothing of Giovanni Giamarco he did not already know. Of the Frosts, however, he wrote, "Not the type of people you want to tangle with, my boy." There followed a long and convoluted account of their latest doings according to the London gossipmongers.

The two were living on tick. They had tried to secure a match for Miss Frost with a peer in Cornwall, a foolish young man who had been caught with her in a most compromising position. The peer's father, a respected member of the House, had threatened to cut off his son's inheritance if any marriage took place. The Frosts had, it was rumored, been granted a lavish financial settlement, with which they had booked passage to Italy, where, it had been hoped, the young lady would snare an Italian, no more to trouble the young men of Great Britain.

On the heels of his father's revealing missive, the ludicrous note from Giovanni was almost amusing.

"You have disgraced a young woman's most precious possession," it read. "Her honor. Declare the means by which we might settle this like gentlemen, as well as the time and place, at your earliest convenience."

A duel over Laura Frost, a gazetted fortune hunter, was not something Reed cared to engage in if he could avoid it. A thought occurred to him. A thought of some brilliance given the circumstances. He retreated to the attic for paper and pen and sat himself down to scribble out his reply.

"I will meet you at noon, the day after tomorrow, on the very spot where you believe Miss Frost's honor was compromised. Weapons to be determined on the spot."

There. That ought to forestall Giovanni's ire, and he would leave town tomorrow. They need never meet. He had far more important problems to deal with than a duel over untrue history.

Chapter Fourteen

It was hopeless! Numbers swam before Reed's eyes in the flickering candlelight. He could feel a headache coming on. His pulse pounded too quickly in his temples. Finished tallying, the sums confirmed his worst fears. He tried to believe the numbers could not be right, that he had miscalculated, dreadfully miscalculated something.

A second tallying offered exactly the same results. His pulse jumped another notch. The sorry truth was, his father's income disappeared far faster than it was produced! His parents were in fearful debt. How could his father write so condescendingly of the Frosts living on tick when he was floundering in the river himself?

Of an inheritance, Reed could find nothing to speak of. He was more likely to inherit a great deal of debt than anything else. So contrary was this to his understanding of the natural order of things, so greatly did this threaten his perception of the future, it left him feeling tetherless, almost bodyless with shock. Hard to grasp the idea, but his father's estate had all but vanished, dwindled away by careless spending, foolhardly investments, and high interests on unnecessary loans!

Gone, all of it gone! With it went the comfortable future he had too long taken for granted. How arrogant to have assumed that things would remain constant, unchanged and secure. How foolish!

He closed his eyes and leaned his head into his hands, his head too heavy for his neck alone to carry. He could not see past it, a financial problem this enormous. It boggled the mind. He had always taken money for granted.

"Reed?" It was Megan's voice floating out of the darkness near the doorway. "Having trouble sleeping?" She looked like a little girl, standing barefoot, nightrail billowing, her hair long and loosely tumbled across the crochet shawl thrown around her shoulders.

"Trouble, yes," he whispered, without going into detail. She looked young and innocent and untroubled. He did not want to burden her with his problem. "Bad dreams?" he hazarded.

"No, not really, just too many thoughts careening around in my head. Do you know what I mean?"

He almost laughed. He knew exactly what she meant, only it was numbers that kept roaming around in his brainpan, and the panicked thoughts that went with them. "Yes, I do."

She picked up a pair of boots that had been left to dry near the fireplace and sat down to slip her feet into them. As she bent over, her nightshift strained against the curve of her buttocks. As she straightened, it strained against the curve of her breast.

"I had it in mind to take a turn in the garden," she said. "I generally take a moonlit stroll in the garden at home when my thoughts will not be still. Care to join me? We are much less likely to wake Gussie and Tom if we talk."

It took him a moment to absorb the words. He forced himself to look away from the shadow of her nipple beneath the pale white fabric as she stood. "Sorry to disappoint, but it is raining."

"Is it?" She opened the door to peer out into the night where a gentle, soundless rain was indeed drenching their surroundings. Quietly closing the door, she returned to the chair. "Has it been raining long?"

"An hour or two." He could not look at her, could not risk his eyes straying in a manner most uncharacteristic of him. "I do have a suggestion, if it's fresh air you are after."

"Yes?" Her hair, like a shower of spilled spice, caught what little light the room possessed when she bent to slip the boots from her feet. Her neck, he thought, had never looked so fragile. He sketched the line of it in the open ledger. A line or two more, and her profile was captured amongst the sums.

"There is a queer little balcony on the south side of my room where we might sit and chat undisturbed."

She turned to look at him, her face flushed from bending, her eyes shining with the rushlight by which he had been working. "The spinning gallery! What a splendid idea."

"Is that what it is called?" Quietly closing the ledger on both his drawing of her and his personal nightmare, he picked up the rush holder and lit their way to the stairs.

There was a difference, he thought, an uneasy difference, between leading Megan upstairs to his study in daylight and in leading her upstairs to the room where he slept in the dead of night. She felt it, too. She would not have hesitated in the doorway else, her eyes wider than usual, dark with expanded pupils.

Rather than study the matter too intently, rather than look at her as she clutched her shawl tightly about her shoulders, he crossed to his bed. "Here, take these!" He tossed her the pillows and gathered up an armful of the bedcoverings before he led the way out of a narrow doorway on the far wall.

The spinning gallery was a long, narrow balcony of sorts tucked up under the overhang of the roof, too shy of headroom to stand upright in properly. One end of it currently sheltered a sweet-smelling stack of the peat that was used in the fireplace downstairs. A high, wooden balustrade railing prevented either of them from pitching into the yard below. Hunchbacked, they arranged the bedding and pillows into a sort of sultan's bower and settled themselves.

There was little room for them to spread out. They were practically in each other's laps when they sat down and looked out over the dripping, glistening landscape behind the house. The smell of wet grass and damp peat was refreshing after the musty, candle-wax closeness of the cottage.

"Was this miserable little space really used for spinning?" he asked, more to break the silence than out of any real desire to know. It was a safe topic.

"Yes. I would think so. I think it must have been the perfect, out-of-the-way spot to set up a spinning wheel."

"All we need is Rumplestiltskin," he said lightly.

She nodded, delighted. "To spin some gold."

The idea appealed to him more than she could know. But it was a fairy-tale solution to a problem all too real.

"The troll would want our firstborn," he reminded her. "Perhaps it is best we do not find him here."

She blushed a deep rose and hugged her shawl tighter around her shoulders.

"What keeps you awake, Megan?"

She pursed her lips. The moonlight on her profile was worthy of recording by an artist of greater skill than he could lay claim to.

"I have been thinking of my own firstborn," she surprised him in saying. "I have been thinking of London, of love, and of marriage."

These were not safe topics. He did not press for details.

She sighed. "What keeps you awake?"

Another unsafe topic, his impending doom. He made light of it. "I have been tallying numbers that do not want to add up."

"Is your father's bookkeeping in a state?"

"The worst," he admitted. He could not admit to her that Lord and Lady Talcott had adopted the habit of living above and beyond their means. "Your thoughts, I daresay, have been far more interesting than mine."

"How so?"

"Love and marriage are far more interesting than finance, surely."

"Additions and subtractions of a different order," she said quietly. Her expression hid in the shadows.

A silence fell between them. Rain drummed in a soothing rattle against the roof. Equally soft, almost as soothing, she asked him, "Money trouble, is it?"

"Yes," he blurted, relieved she had guessed, even more relieved that she had asked. It did not occur to him that she had just avoided explaining her own troubling thoughts of love and marriage. "Stupid really, but I am feeling paralyzed by the whole thing. I vacillate between not wanting to believe there is a problem and the feeling it is a problem so enormous I haven't the slightest idea where to begin dealing with it."

"How enormous is enormous?"

"It is a mountain in my mind."

"Even a mountain is not insurmountable. What are your choices?"

Choices? Did he have any choices?

"I could, like my parents, ignore the problem."

"Ha!" she said. "Not and get any sleep. What else? Come, come! The answers to most our problems stare us in the face if we will only open our eyes to see them."

"I could follow the solicitor's advice."

"Which is?"

"Liquidate and consolidate everything."

"That requires your father's involvement, does it not?"

"Yes. Small chance of that."

"What other options then?"

"I could leave it all behind me. Liquidate my personal belongings for fare to the Americas or the Indies. Start a new life from scratch."

She stretched her hand between the balustrade to

catch a handful of the runoff from the roof. "You could marry into money," she suggested.

He frowned and flung himself into a more comfortable position on the bedding. "I am loath to do that. It was with that end in mind my parents wed."

"Was it really?" She let the water dribble away between outstretched fingers.

He closed his eyes briefly.

"I thought you knew. Father had land, Mother, money. A match made in fiscal heaven. I do not know two more miserable people when they are together. Our current financial crisis is rooted in that misery."

"I had no idea," she said softly, withdrawing her hand from the wet to dry it on his bedclothes. "So which is it? The Americas or the Indies?"

"That requires thought," he murmured.

They fell quiet again, watching the rain fall. Megan rearranged her position on their makeshift pallet, that she might lean against the pillow next to him.

He liked having her close. She smelled sweet and good and familiar. There was comfort in the trust she exhibited curling up so close to him, her eyes closing, her voice drowsing along through a rambling discussion about their combined impressions of the Indies and the Americas. Reed had no idea she was drifting off until her head sank onto his shoulder. Odd, how comforting it was to have the steady warmth of her breath against his neck, the weighty warmth of her head against his shoulder, the airy brush of her hair against his cheek. There was trust inherent in the gesture, even unconsciously made. Reed felt oddly relieved. If Megan had been overly concerned as to his ability to solve his financial crisis, she would never have drifted off to sleep. It occurred to him that he had never allowed her to reveal just what it was that had kept her awake.

He could not bring himself to disturb her, so peaceful was her face, so soft and steady her breathing. Entranced, he cradled the warmth of her. The dark depths of her eyes had been shut away from him—her wonderfully mobile mouth, stilled. How pale and soft was her skin. Her hair smelled like roses. The nutmeg tresses tickled his cheek.

He could see no sense in rousing her, no sense, either, in toting her all the way downstairs to her bed when he might just as easily tuck her into his bed.

"Megan," he whispered, "are you asleep?"

She did not rouse. With great care he picked her up, marveling at the sweet, soft heft of her drowsy body. He was unprepared for the little moan she made, unprepared for the endearing manner in which she snuggled her face into his shirtfront. It occurred to him that given the chance, he would carry this sweet burden with him all the way to the Americas. He forgot how low the ceiling was and cracked his head smartly against one of the beams.

He wanted to shout out "Bloody Hell!" but stifled the impulse. Eyes and mouth squeezed shut, head spinning, he leaned against the door frame, steadying himself, unable to refrain from a volley of heartfelt but whispered "Ow! Ow! Ows!" that in no way began to voice the screaming pain in his head.

Megan did not stir. Oblivious, she slept on. Eyes watering he took care not to smack his head again, took care, too, not to bang Megan's head or shins in carrying her through the doorway to his room. Gently, he lowered her onto his bed. Tenderly, he tucked the coverlet around her. Could he make a new life for himself in America? A life without Megan?

Rubbing at his bruised and throbbing skull, he stood gazing at her. Such an innocent and fragile mite she looked, curled up in the same feather ticking that had so recently enfolded him each night. There was something unexpectedly provocative in thinking that they two shared the same bed, if only on different nights.

So provocative was the thought, it drove him out onto the spinning gallery to collect pillows for her head. In the positioning of those pillows, he touched her cheek lightly with the side of his hand. Like velvet, the plush of her skin felt rich against his knuckles. With that touch came a flood of desire to let his hand remain there, nestled by her cheek, all night long. She stirred however, his touch threatening to wake her. Unable to predict his actions should she wake, he fled the room—fled the seduction of her innocence, her trust, and her flesh soft as velvet.

Downstairs, he crept into the quiet emptiness of the room that was Megan's. It was not so very different from his, but for the fact that her presence hung tangibly about the place in a faint hint of tuberose.

Sitting himself on the bed, he slipped off his walking shoes, setting them neatly on the floor beside a smaller, more feminine pair of shoes. His footwear looked decidedly de trop right next to Megan's. Furtively, he stripped off his clothes and hung them in the wardrobe, draping them far too familiarly over one of Megan's dresses. Half naked, he crept around in the still darkness of the room, convinced that at any moment he would wake Gussie and Tom in the room next door and be discovered.

He found little relief in tucking himself into Megan's bed and wrapping Megan's bedlinens around his bare torso. A stronger whiff of tuberose clung tenaciously to the sheets, undeniably arousing, raising hair, gooseflesh, and unexpectedly carnal thoughts. He had always associated the perfume of the tuberose with Megan without really being conscious of the association. Sinking into the soft feather mattress, he was beset by the strange impression that he sank himself, head to toe, against the softness of Megan's breast. Clutching the pillow, he buried his face in its sweetly scented depths, beseiged with the impression that he clutched at Megan herself. He longed to return to his own bed, and Megan still in it, longed to seek out the precise pulse points where she dabbed the same provocative perfume.

Chapter Fifteen

Megan awoke reluctantly from the most pleasant of dreams. In it, Reed held her gently cradled in his arms. So realistic was the dream, so vibrantly sensual, that she could actually smell Reed's cologne on the sheet tucked under her chin.

The sound of rain against the rooftop was wrong, the very light against her eyelids was wrong, as was the muffled twitter of housemartins at the window and the texture of the mattress beneath her body. Subtle things, but telling.

Her eyes popped open in alarm.

Rain on the roof! She should not be able to hear rain on the roof. She stared in confusion at an unfamiliar ceiling.

She sat up abruptly in Reed's bed! Reed's bed? Heaven help her! What was she doing here? There was no sign of Reed, just his clothes and painting gear. The spinning gallery! Her attention riveted on the little door in the outside wall. The last thing she remembered was sitting outside, on the spinning gallery, talking to Reed. She listened for some sound. There was nary a peep, or a creak, or a breath taken. The shawl she had wrapped around her shoulders last night was folded neatly over the back of a nearby chair. She had no memory of putting it there.

Leaping from the bed she swung the shawl around her shoulders and dashed from the room. With quick, furtive steps, she crept down the stairs, thanking her stars that the stairs did not creak too loudly and feeling blessed that Tom and Gussie had yet to rise.

What had transpired the night before? Beyond a certain point, events were a complete blank. She certainly had no memory of climbing into Reed's bed. Wild thoughts whirled through her mind. What had possessed her to stay in his room the entire night?

It never occurred to her that Reed might have swapped sleeping arrangements with her because she had fallen asleep. Her mind was too caught up in more provocative scenarios. Flustered, she burst into her room, closed the door behind her and flung herself upon the bedcovers, only to discover with a startled squeal that the bed was not empty, as she had assumed. It did, in fact, writhe with life. She had landed directly on top of someone, a suddenly animated someone.

"Hallo!" Reed exclaimed, popping up from the bedlinens like a bleary-eyed, bare-chested jack-in-the-box.

"Heavens!" she cried.

Three things flashed through her mind. First, Reed appeared to have nothing on beneath the sheets. Second, the moving limb beneath her hip must be his leg. She certainly hoped it was his leg. And third, she had never seen Reed in need of a shave, as he desperately needed one now.

"What are you doing here?" they bleated in unison.

A thump from the room next door as a pair of feet hit the floor. "Megan?" A querulous voice called from the other side of the wall.

"Gussie!" Megan breathed, even as Reed echoed the name, his face a picture of panic.

A pounding of footsteps in the hall, Megan threw the bedlinens over Reed's head and the door burst open to reveal Augusta, her nightcap askew, her expression one of alarm.

Megan hopped hastily from the bed.

In so doing, she accidently kneed Reed in the stomach. He gave a little groan.

"Megan!" Augusta gasped. "Dear God, what have you gone and done?"

"Done?" Megan repeated. "I've done nothing."

Reed popped his head above the covers and calmly agreed. "Looks far worse than it is, you see. I do assure you, we have done nothing to be ashamed of."

"Nothing! You call hiding in my sister's bed nothing?" Her voice rose with every word. "Heaven's name, Reed Talcott, you get out of there this instant. Do you hear me? Get out, or I shall drag you out."

"You don't want to do that." Reed held up one hand and with the other drew the coverlet more closely around his bare torso.

"Oh don't I?"

"I do assure you."

Gussie grabbed his hand with startling strength and gave a sturdy yank. It was a good thing he had hold of the bedclothes else he would have tumbled from the bed to the floor completely in the altogether. He landed with a crash, a flailing tangle of legs and linens.

"How dare you defile my little sister!" Gussie thundered.

"What!" Reed exclaimed.

"No, Gussie!" Megan cried. "It's not what you think."

"Oh no! What is this then, that he should be in your bed without a stitch of clothing to cover him?"

"What the devil is going on?" Tom appeared, looking rather more tousled than usual. Spying Reed, his eyebrows shot up. "Oho!" he said. "What have we here?"

"Nothing . . ." Megan tried to explain.

"Tom, you must throw him out of the house immediately," Gussie ordered.

"Must he?" Reed said.

"Outside? In the rain?" Tom asked.

"No! Tom, there is no call for anything so rash." Megan could not seem to make herself heard.

"At once!" Gussie was adamant.

"That might prove a trifle hasty, my love. You must

allow Reed a moment, at the very least, to make himself decent."

"It takes more than clothing to make a man decent," Gussie snapped. Holding her hand out to Megan, she said, "Come, We will leave this to Tom."

"But you have it all wrong . . ."

"Come, Megan," Gussie insisted, turning on her heel. "You have some explaining to do."

"If you will only listen, that is exactly what I have been trying to do," Megan said petulantly. She followed her sister to the sitting room, which smelled damply of the rain because two of the windows had been left open.

Gussie closed the door behind them and leaned against it, her arms folded across her chest. "All right. What have you to say for yourself? Are you ruined?"

"I am not ruined," Megan said emphatically. "Nor was I ever in any danger of same."

"But Reed was naked and in your bed!" Gussie crossed the room to snap shut the windows.

"And I was in his bed."

"In his?" Gussie sat down abruptly on the settee. "Dear God. Father will have my head for this. How often have you spent the night together then?"

"Together?" Megan, shocked, sat down beside her sister. "We haven't!"

Gussie leapt up from the settee to pace the room, her bedrail flapping about her ankles, the braid in which she confined her hair swaying at her waist. "Don't lie to me, Megan. Can you honestly tell me he has not touched you, or forced himself upon you, that he has not compromised you beyond redemption?"

"Yes. I can honestly say Reed has not touched me, much less forced himself upon me. Reed slept in my bed because I was safely tucked into his. I must have fallen asleep out on the spinning gallery."

"The gallery?"

"Yes. We went there to talk."

"That's all you did? Talk?"

"Yes. Oh, Gus, more's the pity, he never so much as kissed me."

Gussie stopped her pacing.

"He had every opportunity. We were quite alone."

She sank down on the settee. "I am relieved."

"Yes," Megan said wistfully, tracing with her finger one of the needlepoint patterns in the upholstery. "You need never fear for my honor or virtue in Reed's company. He does not love me in that way."

"But you do. You are still in love with him, aren't you? I thought you had long since outgrown the infatuation."

Megan felt like crying. Pressing her lips together, she fought the impulse and nodded. "Yes, well, I have tried very hard not to love Reed. It has been my intention from the beginning that our time together here at the Lakes should be my farewell to such feelings. And yet, I am a miserable failure, Gus. You see, I wish he would touch me, or kiss me—something—just once, before I put all such thoughts and feelings behind me."

"Poor Meg." Gussie opened her arms.

Megan fell against her sister's shoulder. Augusta smelled of warm muslin and Tom. "Oh, Gussie, I have never been more miserable, and without the slightest notion what to do about it."

"I know." Gussie rocked her in her arms.

"Do you?" Megan moaned. "Can you? You have Tom."

"I did not always have Tom. In fact, I made myself quite miserable over a lad in London who cared nothing at all for me."

Megan drew back to stare at her sister in surprise. "Did you? Who? What did you do about him?"

Gussie smoothed Megan's hair away from her face.

"He was a handsome and personable young man I met at the very beginning of my Season in London. I have never mentioned his name to you, or to Mother and Father. In fact, I have not mentioned him to Tom.

"Did it end badly then?"

"It ended with a kiss."

"A kiss?"

"Yes. My first. It was a dreadful kiss. I knew after that one kiss that there was nothing between us and never would be."

"A kiss can be that telling?"

"Absolutely. Perhaps all that is needed to end your infatuation with Reed is to ask him to kiss you."

"Gussie!" Megan was shocked.

"Megan!" Gussie smiled mischievously. "You will not be ruined by a kiss, any more than by sleeping in Reed's bed as long as he is not in it."

Explanations and apologies made and accepted all around, the truth of the bed business unraveled itself. Reed was not thrown from the house. He could not even leave for home on his own accord, as had been his intention. The roads were too wet. The rain continued unceasingly to fall, making a muddy mess of everything. It was noon before the skies began to clear. Reed postponed his plans to leave until the following day and it was decided that there was no better opportunity for viewing Stock Ghyll Force, than in the aftermath of the rain.

Megan and Reed set out together on rented hacks to have a look.

"Is it to be India, or the Americas?" Megan had to ask. She kneed her mount up beside Reed's, troubled by the idea that he meant not only to leave her, but to go so far away.

He looked puzzled by her question, as if the matter had slipped his mind entirely. "What? Oh. I have yet to decide. I must say, I am surprised your sister chose not to come with us. After this morning's contretemps I had the feeling she would never allow us another moment alone together."

Megan nodded, her mind still caught on the thought that he must one day leave her. With this second mention of Gus her gaze was irresistibly drawn to Reed's lips. "She feels guilty about the awful things she said to you this morning."

Reed shifted his weight. The saddle creaked. "Really! But I understood completely how the wrong impression was to be had. Why should that keep her and Tom away?"

"They mean to prove to you their restored confidence in your intentions as far as I am concerned."

"Oh!" From his expression it was clear he had never anticipated their distrust. "A pity really, that they decided not to come."

"Oh?" Did he not care at all to be alone with her? Did it mean nothing to him? Did the thought that he must one day leave her never trouble him?"

"I would imagine we are going to see Stock Ghyll Force at its very best today."

He was right, of course. The best of Stock Ghyll Force could be heard long before they saw it—water hurling itself with resounding force over stone. The sound drew them, demanding their attention the closer they got to it, filling their ears with the rush, rush, rush of what would seem to be an endless source of water. Megan's worries were drowned in the noise. The Force completely captured her imagination.

On foot, the horses tethered at a nearby inn, they saw it piecemeal through the trees, a flash of boiling white among the green. The rain-fed trickle had become a force to be reckoned with, a force of romantic proportions. Water foamed and sparkled, churned and pulsed over the top of the hill above—throwing itself three times down the incline and over dark boulders, like wet whalebacks, before it plunged into a pool at the base of the ninety-foot tumble and becalmed itself.

They stood still a moment, oblivious to the drizzle of rain, staring.

"It's marvelous," Reed exclaimed as he peered

through his spattered Claude glass. He had to shout to be heard above the noise.

Speechless, she nodded.

"Do you care to have a look?" He offered the glass. "It puts a whole new perspective on things."

She shook her head and began to say something he could not hear. When he did not understand a word of it and begged her to repeat herself, she grabbed his lapel, leaned close, and cupping her hand, said directly into his ear, "Your glass, it tends to distance and dwarf everything." Her breath was hot against his skin. The tilt of her bonnet sent a chill dribble of rain down the back of his neck.

She smelled of tuberose, damp tuberose.

She spread one arm toward the waterfall, as if to embrace it and draw it near. "I have no desire to distance myself from it," she said. Her breath tickled his ear. He closed his eyes, losing himself in the fervor of her words. "It fills me: eyes, ears, lungs. My very heart is touched by the essence of waterfall. I feel wet, and wild and reckless. Do you feel it?"

Her question had an unexpected urgency. Reed opened his eyes. There was a wild and natural beauty about Megan in this moment—a beauty he had never recognized in her before. There was a damp, curling glisten to her—an almost feral sheen. Hair and skin, eyes and lips, all seemed touched by the moment.

She lifted her face to the drizzling rain and let it kiss her cheek. Reed felt awed in witnessing such abandonment. He felt a trifle panicked, a trifle jealous. He had never experienced the merging with nature she described, no matter how beautiful the scene spread before him, and there had, in the course of his travels, been beauty beyond measure offered up to his eyes. He had framed all, tamed all, in his Claude glass. She was right. It made manageable raw beauty that might otherwise overwhelm. Without the glass setting boundaries, he had the feeling he might have been swept away any number of times by beauty. He was a gentleman, an English gentleman. He had never allowed himself to succumb—to what he was not sure, but like the helpless, tumbling splash of the water before him, he felt he had no control over where such passion might take him.

"How wonderful to be a waterfall," Megan breathed. She let go of his lapel, but made no move to step away from him. He could count the very beads of moisture on her eyelashes. Eyes, hair, lips, there was a dampness to all of her. By God, she was beautiful! He would like to capture her in conte crayon and vine charcoal.

"We will not be able to draw or paint today. It is far too wet." His voice sounded unused—rusty.

She did not seem to notice. "Perhaps that is a blessing. We are forced to enjoy the very ephemeral nature of beauty. There is an added piquancy by its very transience."

He could not agree with her more. For the moment they shared, the sounds, sights, and smells, the very closeness of their stance. It was a moment that would pass. He did not want it to pass. He wanted to hold on to it, to hold on to the beauty of her. She would be gone from him soon. She might be gone forever.

"Shall we look for cover?" she asked.

For an instant, her words made no sense to him.

She tipped back her head to gaze at the ceiling of leaves above their heads, her mouth twisting in the impish manner that he found so endearing. "It sounds as if the rain has begun to fall harder."

She was right. The rain began to fall in earnest, threatening to soak them to the skin, even as she spoke. With a squeal, she grasped his damp hand in hers. Together they ran for the nearest cover.

Chapter Sixteen

They found shelter beneath a sprawling, open-sided coppice barn attached to a mill. Several mills took advantage of the tumbling power of falling water that Stock Beck gathered in the heights of Red Scree Fell. This particular mill made bobbins. From its doors spilled light, noise, sawdust, and the faintly astringent odor of freshly cut wood. In unspoken agreement, Megan and Reed skirted the doorway and headed away from the noises of sawing and drilling, away from the rumbling vibrations of the line shaft with its rows of flapping belts. They chose, instead, to wind their way through birch, ash, sycamore, and hazel wood. Stack after neat stack of varying sizes of the same sort of straight, limbless, coppice wood they had watched being cut only a few days prior. They came to a stop in a dripping corner where they could watch the mill wheel and listen to its soothing, sluicing creak.

In the turning wheel, in the very falling of the rain, Megan saw time passing. Life, like the river, rushed past her with every breath she took. Did a life beset by troubles, she wondered, speed up like the flow of the river beset by rain?

The door to the mill creaked open, thrown wide by two men laden with swill baskets piled high with finished bobbins.

"Come!" Reed grabbed her arm, pulling her into the narrow space between two stacks of stripped poles, his finger to his lips.

The space was tight. Megan found herself pressed against Reed, staring at the beat of the pulse in his neck. With every breath she took her breasts grazed against the lapels of his coat. With every breath he took, the hair on her brow was stirred.

The mill door creaked again. The men had finished their task. Reed released her, pushed past her, bringing them for a moment, hip to hip, knee to knee, his chest to hers. It was now or never, Megan thought. She must, in some way, convince Reed to kiss her. But how to do so, when he did not seem to notice the touch of their bodies? He was staring toward the mill door.

"They would doubtless have assumed we required a tour of the mill," he said. "I would much rather stay here, watching the rain. I thought you would agree."

She did agree. There was much she would discuss with him.

"What do you see when you look at me?" she asked.

He tried to laugh away her question. "What do I see? Whatever do you mean?"

"What do you think I mean? You have, over the past few days, expounded at length on what you see in the landscape. Please turn the same discerning eyes on me and tell me what you see."

They still stood almost on top of one another between the piles of wood. Too close, perhaps, for such a question. He would not look at her other than in uneasy sideways glances. "This is silly."

"Indulge me, please. I must know."

He faced her abruptly. "What would you have me see, Nutmeg? I see you."

"What about me do you see?" There was an unusual tension between them.

Perhaps he felt as trapped as she by their close proximity now that he looked at her. Stepping free from their cramped hiding place, he dipped his hand into his pocket. Pulling out his folio of Claude glasses, he turned to observe her from a distance.

"Without benefit of the glass, if you please," she said.

He pocketed the glass. Without it, he seemed unable to gaze at her for any length of time. He did in fact seem embarrassed by her question. "I see the imp—the girl I grew up with, the young woman I enjoy painting with as long as she does not trouble me overmuch with absurd questions."

"Is that all?" She was disappointed.

He stopped looking at her, concentrating his attention instead on peeling bits of bark from one of the poles that protruded a little from the nearest stack of birch wood. "I've no idea what else you want me to say."

Megan emerged from their hiding place. "I do not want you to *say* anything in particular. I just want to know that you see me, that you have scrutinized me with the same intensity and concentration that you devote to the landscapes you paint."

He abandoned his bark picking with a baffled look. He shifted from one foot to the other uneasily, and ran his hand through his damp hair.

"Shall I tell you what I see in you?" she asked.

"You see a sadly rain-drenched fellow with muddy boots and bark bits in his hair."

She smiled and shook her head. "I see nothing of the kind. It is my dearest friend I notice, not the condition of his boots. I see, too, an obedient son, a well-mannered English gentleman, an intelligent, orderly thinker, a quiet, reserved young man with an eye for beauty and both the talent and desire to collect and record his interpretation of that beauty. I see the boy I grew up with when you smile. You should smile more often, Reed. You have the most delightful dimples. I see, in your eyes, a kindred spirit. I see . . . a hidden sadness, too, behind the smiles and beneath your quiet reserve—and now worry—which I have never known to trouble you before. I see Reed Talcott, a young man whom I admire, trust and care for, whom I . . ."

Love, she would have said, but he interrupted her.

"Stop! Stop! My head is so big by now that it will require a wheelbarrow to trundle it home again if you add so much as another thimbleful of praise. I had no idea there was so much in me to see."

"You do not know yourself as well as you should then."

Her words seemed to have impact. He made a face. "Perhaps not."

He seemed prepared to look at her now, but so intense was his gaze, so complete his perusal that she had trouble maintaining eye contact. She could think of nothing but Gussie's talk of kisses when she did, so she studied her shoes instead. They were muddy, as was the hem of her gown.

She could not recall a time when Reed had examined her so keenly, his eyes passing over her slowly from head to toe. The intensity of his unswerving examination was unnerving.

"Well?" she said when the moment seemed to have stretched interminably long with nothing to relieve the silence but the creak of the mill wheel and the pelting of rain against the roof.

"What do I see?" He seemed willing to look at any part of her now, as long as it did not involve looking her directly in the eyes. "I see my friend Megan Breech, with hair the color of freshly ground nutmeg and skin the color of cream."

So unexpected was his poetic approach she burst out laughing. "Am I an eggnog?"

He frowned and turned away. "This is not easy. Do you want to hear me out, or not?"

"I do. Silly of me to laugh. Please forgive me. I will refrain from any more judgmental noises or commentary."

Uneasily he faced her again and cleared his throat. "I see a female with pleasing looks, symmetrically arranged. The landscape of her, uh . . . your body, has changed. There are more hills and valleys." He stopped and threw up his hands. "I am no good at this."

She stifled all amusement. He was trying so very hard. "Go on. You are doing fine."

He took a deep, determined breath and faced her again, his gaze so firmly engaging hers she could not look away. "The little girl I grew up beside has disappeared almost entirely." He sounded as if it saddened him. "I see her peeping through on occasion, but for the most part, in the place of that child stands a young woman whose mind, motives, and movements I can no longer predict—as much as I would like to. The young woman I see is beautiful, creative, and intelligent. I adore her sense of fun, her keen perceptiveness. While she is well-mannered and ladylike, her finesse is tempered by an unaffected naturalness that is sure to win her many friends in London. I see an openness of mind, spirit, and heart that I would myself lay claim to if it were in my nature. I see you, Megan, and every time I do, of late, I find myself awed by Nature's hand."

Enchanted into an almost breathless state while he spoke, she inhaled sharply the clean, pungent smell of wet wood. She would have said something had their magical moment of rain-draped solitude not been cut short by the appearance of three lads, their hair silted with sawdust. They came pelting into the coppice barn to fetch wood, stopping short when they realized there were strangers in the barn.

The tallest of the four called out, "Who are you, then?"

"Time for our tour," Reed said softly.

Megan, still speechless, nodded.

Reed stepped forward to speak to the lads.

She stood, dumbstruck, her ears deaf to all but the memory of his words. She did not regain the use of either ears or tongue until Reed indicated that they were to follow the lads into the mill.

"Reed," she said, and when he turned to her, eyebrows raised inquisitively, she said softly, "Thank you."

"What for?"

"For what you said. It was beautiful."

He nodded, smiled, and said lightly, "Come on then, we've the workings of a mill to examine."

The rain had stopped by the time they emerged from the sawdust-infested, noise-driven world of Horrax's bobbin mill. The tour had been fascinating, and deafening. The still, rain-pearled beauty of the birch trees, ferns, and wild cress as they headed back along the dripping, moss-scented pathway was almost overwhelming by comparison. The absence of noise other than the twittering of a willow warbler seemed huge to Megan. She had to fill it.

"You willingly kissed Miss Frost the other night, didn't you?"

"What?" Her question took him by surprise.

"I have turned the thing over and over in my mind. To my way of thinking, that is the only way she could have gotten hold of your tongue the way she did."

He cleared his throat. "You are the inquisitive one today."

"Yes. I am right, am I not?"

"Well"—he broke off a reddish stalk of ragged robin and plucked the individual flower heads one by one, so that a trail of tiny blossoms was left in their wake—"it started out as willing. She fairly threw herself at me, you see, and no graceful way to avoid her advances. She has been throwing herself in my way quite a bit of late. I thought it would be a bit of rudeness to turn her off yet again."

"Rudeness. Hmm. Have you kissed many girls, Reed?"

"That would be telling."

"More than one?"

"Why do you ask? You should not ask me such things!"

"If not you, Reed, whom shall I ask?"

"You should not ask at all. Why the sudden interest in kissing? Has Giovanni dared to kiss you, pet? Has Burnham?"

"No, but I have been talking to Gussie about my coming out and about marriage and the duties of being a wife. She mentioned kissing among other things. She said there will be those among my suitors who will try to steal them."

"I hope she told you, too, that you must discourage such liberties."

As they were approaching Stock Ghyll Force, Megan was compelled to raise her voice. "She did, but then she admitted that kissing the right fellow is quite pleasant. She said I must be sure that my first kiss was carefully allotted. She said it could be most unpleasant if one was not discriminating. Her own first experience was quite dreadful."

"Dear, dear. I am surprised she tells you so much." Reed was speaking at the top of his lungs.

"But of course she tells me everything of importance when she thinks I am ready for the hearing of it. We are sisters. Anyway, Gussie said she would much rather her first kiss had been with someone she knew, cared for, and trusted. So great and negative an impression did it leave on her memory, that I am determined my first kiss shall be with someone I care for dearly. Someone who will, with gentle patience, show these inexperienced lips just how the thing is done."

"Lucky fellow!" he cried. The increasing din of the water threatened to overwhelm their conversation.

She grabbed his arm and shouted, though it felt odd to be shouting such a remark, "There is only one gentleman I trust for such a task."

"Who?" he shouted back.

She said nothing, merely looked at him, hoping he

would understand. She had to know what lay between them. She had to know in order to move on. It was time to move on—to foster affections for some other man, but she had no desire to carry with her regrets of what might have been. She said nothing, therefore, hoping he would comprehend.

His head reared back like that of a startled horse. "Are you saying you wish *me* to kiss you?" he screamed at her.

"Who else?" she shouted, and it struck her that this was not the sort of conversation one should be conducting at the top of one's lungs.

"I was sure you must be referring to Giovanni."

"Should I ask him instead?"

Reed shook his head. "By no means," he bellowed.

In as dispassionate a shout as she could muster, she asked, "Do you refuse me, then? Or will you oblige?"

"You are serious?"

She could not let him see just how serious. Her gaze dropped away from his. "Is it too much to ask?"

He licked his lips, a sign of uneasiness, but rather than continue to shout at her he leaned in close to her ear to say, "I am afraid my kisses may disappoint."

She drew back from the breathy caress of his voice to look him in the eye. "Disappoint? How so? Are you an inferior kisser?"

"No!" He was shouting again. She had offended him. She could hear how offended he was in his tone. She could see it in his frown. "It's just that I am afraid a kiss between us might prove passionless."

Passionless? That he should assume them passionless, stung. Had he expected passion of Miss Frost, she wondered, before she bit into him?

She beckoned him closer with a crook of her finger. Standing on tiptoe, one hand to steady her on the flat of his chest, she lifted her lips to speak directly into his ear. "Would you mind pretending?"

He was frowning again when she pulled back to examine his reaction.

"And you?" he asked, his face troublingly close. "Could you pretend?"

She laughed, sure her face must be a telling scarlet color, and shouted, "You need not worry about my feelings."

"But I do worry," he said, and as he did not bother to shout she almost did not hear the words over the rush of the Force.

Did he know? she wondered. Had he known all along how foolishly she doted on him? Had he simply ignored her feelings, hoping she would grow out of them, hoping she would mature enough to realize the futility of plain Miss Breech falling in love with the heir of Talcott Keep? The idea was humiliating. Her face blazed like an oven. She ducked her chin, hoping against hope he would not notice her discomfort.

"Never mind, then," she said. "I've no desire to twist your arm."

"Pardon?" he asked, leaning closer so that his cheek grazed hers. "What was that last thing you said? I did not hear." His nose was practically in her ear, his every word tickling its inner recesses.

Her eyes closed, the better to savor the smooth touch of his cheek against hers and the rain-drenched smell of the cologne that hung about his person. Her breath faster than usual, she gathered herself together to repeat the horrible words. "Never mind, then. I've no desire . . ." The rest of her words were stopped in her mouth, stopped by the brush of first his cheek, then his lips against hers.

"Are you sure you've no desire?" he whispered, the hot silk of his breath tingling along the sensitive flesh of her lips. Without waiting for her answer, he turned his head, that his mouth might more perfectly match hers.

She tensed, stiffened further when one of his hands made its way around her waist to the small of her back while the other braced her shoulders, drawing her deeper into the warm haven of his arms.

The kiss lasted for no more than a fraction of a moment, and yet so much was she swept away by their bonding heat that when Reed began to pull away, body and mouth, she seemed bent on following him.

Embarrassed, she regained her equilibrium and dared to slide a sideways look at Reed. "Oh!" she said softly. "Oh my!"

Gussie had been wrong. Her first kiss had not diminished in any way her feelings for Reed. It had, in fact, enhanced them. It was going to be harder than ever to turn away from her love for him.

His gaze held a softness, an openness she was not used to seeing. "Your first kiss, Megan. Did you find it in any way disappointing?"

Solemnly she nodded.

His eyes widened. His hand fell away from the small of her back. "How so?"

"It was over far too quickly," she said, horribly disappointed that what she had so long yearned for was so soon finished.

"What?" He pointed to his ears, indicating he had not been able to hear her. Standing on tiptoe, she grasped his shirtpoints, pulling him toward her. She had a fleeting image of his look of surprise—of raised eyebrows, wide eyes, and parted lips. She directed her mouth toward his and closed her eyes, her hands sliding up and around his neck to grasp the hair at the nape of his neck.

Her touch bound them in a way that had never been bound before. With an unexpected groan, Reed grabbed at her waist once more while the humid warmth of his mouth sought hers hungrily, stealing her breath away. Deliriously, she tightened her clasp around his neck, intoxicated by the warm friction of his lips against hers.

The kiss she demanded of him, tender and gently insistent, was perfect—all that she had expected and more. Every iota of her being focused on an awareness of the moment—a shining, breathless, heartbreaking mountain of a moment—a high point from which she could look down on the amazing potential of the landscape of her love for Reed. She would cherish its brief, pulse-racing perfection.

She sighed, swept up in purely hedonistic pleasure, her mouth dewed with kisses, her head filled with the sound of water purling over stone.

He surprised her again. His tongue darted out, a surprising wet warmth, teasing her lips apart.

She drew back in alarm. "What are you doing?"

His face was crimson. "Uhm . . . the French . . . uhm, kiss differently."

"Is this what you were doing with Miss Frost?"

He nodded. "You are not revolted, are you?"

"No. Merely surprised."

"Shall we try again?" He leaned forward.

She leaned back. "We need not, if you find this tiresome."

He laughed, his lips hovering scant inches from hers, his eyes shining like clear blue lakes, so close she could see herself reflected there. She had never felt such a connection between them as was bridged by their gaze. "Tiresome?" he said with a smile, his breath hot and sweet against the sensitized surface of her mouth. "Not at all."

An uncontrollable shiver swept over her. She made no response other than to lift her chin, her lips slightly parted.

His mouth met hers, like old friends, no hesitation now, no holding back. His tongue, given permission, damply plumbed the depths of her mouth, the feeling wild, wet, and out of control. She drank him in, as if she meant to swallow the force of him, her lips demanding the pressure, the damp warmth, the erotic taste. Her hands found their way around his neck. His bound her closer to him at the waist. Knees going weak, her head seemed to fill with the rushing sound of falling water. As if she stood poised at the top of the waterfall, with the meeting of their flesh she dove over the precipice, tumbling, falling, sliding into liquid warmth. The rush of Stock Ghyll Force matched the wild rush of emotion that swept her, head to toe. Megan abandoned herself to the raging of the Force and long-suppressed emotions.

Some dimly suffused part of her brain registered the thought that she must not grow too attached to this incredible, all-consuming sensation. She knew it would not last. Reed meant to go to the Americas.

She never expected to be wrenched from Reed's arms!

It was Giovanni who rudely tore them apart. He stood glowering at Reed, wet from the recent rain, looking more the river god than ever, but for his heightened color and the vein that pulsed purple in his temple. He bellowed, "At it again, are you? You really must learn to display better manners where the young ladies are concerned."

As he shouted the recommendation, Giovanni swung Reed by his lapels, in a half circle, mercilessly directing his footsteps. Into the pool at the bottom of Stock Ghyll Force Reed plunged.

He came up spluttering. "Good God, man! That was entirely uncalled-for."

Both men were shouting. Even without the noise of the Force they would have shouted.

Giovanni shook his finger like a disappointed nanny. "Do you mean to ruin yet another young woman's reputation?"

"No, Giovanni. You have it all wrong." Megan tried to get his attention.

Giovanni ignored her. Stonily he extended a hand to help Reed from the water. They faced one another, both dripping with what seemed a personification of their rage. "The duel, sir!" Giovanni shouted.

"Duel?" Megan exclaimed. "What duel?"

Both gentlemen ignored her.

"Beg pardon," Reed shouted politely. "Slipped my mind."

"Name your weapons." There was little that was polite in Giovanni's tone.

"Weapons?" Reed was trying to remove his drenched jacket and having a spot of trouble, so tightly did the fabric cling.

"Pistols, swords, or fists?" Giovanni demanded.

Chapter Seventeen

M egan was beside Reed in an instant. "A duel?" she
shouted against the noise of the falling water,
against her own disbelief.

Reed fought to extricate himself from his coat, a well-
tailored garment so completely soaked it did not want to
be removed. "Help me off with this thing!" He whirled
in a frustrated circle, arms pinned behind him by coat-
sleeves he had turned almost inside out in an effort to
shed the dripping garment.

"Pistols! Swords! Are you gone mad?" Her voice rose
angrily.

"It is this coat drives me mad. Help me free of it, if
you will."

"We must go at this from the proper direction," she
scolded. The duel concerned her far more than the coat.
"You could be killed or clapped in irons engaging in
such foolishness."

"You assume I would survive the encounter." He managed, at last, to slide free of the sausage-casing sleeves.
Waving the dripping garment at Giovanni, who was as
trapped in the removal of his coat as Reed had been, he
shouted without rancour, "I do not think survival likely,
given his physique."

"You cannot mean to fight him," Megan bellowed.

Giovanni had the look of a man who won any fight in
which he engaged. His seams were in the process, even
now, of giving way under his well-muscled assault.

Reed shrugged.

Megan was infuriated by that shrug. "Perhaps you could strike him down while his arms are pinned."

Reed looked shocked. "You jest!"

"Of course I jest," she yelled. With a feeling of complete frustration she went to assist Giovanni.

He was a single-minded fellow. Over her head he shouted the only question that seemed to trouble his mind. "Pistols, swords, or fists?"

Reed shrugged and headed in the direction of Ambleside. Giovanni and Megan—still mutually fighting his coat—caught up to him, at a pace that had Megan quite breathless.

"You would run from me?" Giovanni shouted.

Reed said with admirable nonchalance, "I do not run. I walk away from the noise. I am tired of shouting. As to your question, I have yet to make up my mind as to weapons, but I should like to be dry before I die. Can we agree upon that much?"

Giovanni, squelching with his every step, reluctantly agreed.

They adjourned to the nearest inn.

Reed was playing for time. He had no idea what weapons to choose against Giovanni, who was his physical superior in every way. He was not so sure he had any intellectual edge over the fellow either, not when he had just been wrenched from the mind-numbing wonder of Megan's lovemaking.

He turned to look at her as they wetly made their way toward dry clothes and a stiff drink. She gazed back with a worried look. Was she as concerned as he that they might never be able to finish their kissing lesson if he went and got himself killed? It behooved him to think of surviving. Perhaps when he was dry, a fitting method would come to him.

And yet, even dry, and more comfortably attired in some of the innkeeper's ill-fitting togs, he had no clear answer. "Best bring me pen and ink," he said to the man as his wet things were taken away.

"Will you be needing to write a letter then, sir?"

"Not a letter, but a document of some importance."

"Yes, sir. Right away, sir."

Reed stopped his departure in the doorway. "Tell me, my good fellow, if you had the choice, would you prefer to die from a fatal thrust, a bloody great hole blown in some part of your anatomy, or a bruising blow to the kidneys?"

The innkeeper looked at him as if he were daft. "I would prefer to die in bed, sir, at a ripe old age, if it's all the same to you."

"As would I." Reed nodded his approval. "How best to go about it is the real question."

"To that, sir, I have no answer. Shall I bring the writing materials here, or do you mean to join your friends downstairs?"

Reed shrugged. "I suppose I shall have to join them eventually. Downstairs will do."

Giovanni was pacing the private sitting room they had been given use of, when Reed made his way downstairs. Megan sat looking out of the mullioned window, hugging herself. He wondered if she was damp, perhaps even a little cold. Her face, paler than usual, turned in his direction the minute he passed through the doorway. It was terror that troubled her, not a chill. He could see it in her eyes despite the weak smile she managed to send him. He wanted to kiss her stiffly upturned lips, wanted to pick up the delightful exchange Giovanni had so rudely interrupted. Far more fun, after all, kissing Megan, warming away her fears, than getting oneself killed.

"Name your weapons." Giovanni was tiresome in his persistence.

Reed took a deep breath. How to convince a hot-blooded Italian bent on his destruction that it was in neither of their best interests to indulge in such barbaric exercise?

"Reed! You cannot go through with this." Megan voiced the very thought that ran through his head.

Giovanni eyed them with bright-eyed expectancy. He looked ready to spring into the active pursuit of a pair of pistols or swords, given the word.

The innkeeper arrived, ink standish and quills balanced on a tray. Giovanni plucked one of the quills from the standish as the man passed him.

"What's this? An instrument of torture?"

"I'll have none of that, now," the innkeeper said. "No stains on the rugs, upholstery, or the shirts I've been kind enough to loan you gents, if you please."

"We shall try to avoid bleeding on anything, if at all possible," Reed said.

"Bleeding? Is it ink do you mean, sir?"

"That, too," Reed said.

Giovanni dismissed the wide-eyed man with a coin and a wave of his hand.

Sharpening a quill, Reed sat at the secretary, pen poised over the inkwell. How did one begin? Ah, yes, he remembered now. "I, Reed Talcott, being of sound mind and body, do hereby bequeath . . ."

Megan leaned in over his elbow, read the words he had written, and hissed, "Stop this nonsense at once."

"I suppose you are right," Reed muttered. One had to possess something of value in order to will it away.

Giovanni leaned heavily on the secretary and threw the quill he had been holding into the standish, splashing ink. "Name your weapons, sir."

Like a bloody parrot he was.

"Name them at once."

A bloody serious parrot. His blue eyes were chill.

"No more prevarication."

Reed looked from Giovanni's implacable expression to the discarded quill. "A pen, sir, shall be your weapon."

"You make a joke, yes?" Giovanni was not amused.

"To the contrary. What better way to voice your contempt of me?"

Megan seemed to hold her breath.

Giovanni shook his head, dashing hope. "The contest does not seem severe enough."

Reed puzzled a moment. "If I cannot convince you of my innocence in the course of a single page, I give you leave to release your version of events to the London papers. No reprisals. No claims of slander."

"Reed," Megan gasped.

"My reputation would be completely ruined. Severe enough for you?"

Giovanni nodded curtly. "I agree to your terms."

Reed smiled, pleased. Life was good. A duel of words, he had a chance of winning.

Half an hour and a scattering of ink-stained sheets later, the pens stopped the erratic scratching that had grated so insistently at Megan's nerves. The silence was more ominous than the scraping of pens. Written pages exchanged, the real test of wills began.

She had contained herself and her tongue far longer than she might have considered possible. Never before had she felt so cut off from what transpired before her very eyes. Designated the outsider in this stupid duel of words, she would go mad if her ignorance went on much longer.

"Ha!" Giovanni said contemptuously before he reached the end of the page.

His contempt did not bode well.

"Mmmm." Reed shook his head over Giovanni's writing. "My, my. That's harsh."

Giovanni angrily waved the page. "You cannot expect me to believe this."

Reed had every appearance of remaining unperturbed. "Read on." He waved his hand negligently. "Do me the courtesy of reading all of it before you make up your mind."

Giovanni read on. Megan got up from the windowseat

to pace the room, fretting. She could see in her mind the awful damage that would come of Giovanni's story being printed in the gossip sheets. Reed would be an outcast—polite society's pariah.

Giovanni stopped reading. With an oath, he cast the page across the surface of the secretary. "This is true?" He slapped at the paper in wide-eyed disbelief. "All of it, true?"

This was not the response Megan had anticipated.

Reed nodded gravely. "I regret to say, it is true, as far as I know. The names and addresses I have included at the bottom of the page should satisfactorily verify my accusations."

"Accusations?" Megan looked on in confusion.

Giovanni stood and held out his hand to Reed. "I owe you an apology."

Megan had to sit down. The room was spinning.

Reed gave Giovanni's outstretched hand a firm shake. "Apology accepted."

Snatching up the pages he had scrawled, Giovanni held the edges of the paper to the candle on the desk. "This insulting bit of slander is best consigned to the flame." The pages caught fire, curling darkly as Giovanni turned and tossed them into the cold fireplace. "I owe you a debt of gratitude," he said earnestly as he turned again to face Reed, his posture more formal than usual. "If there is any way in which I can repay you, you will let me know?"

Reed nodded with subdued enthusiasm. "I will. You are most kind. I am pleased we were able to settle this like gentlemen without bloodshed or blows. In such an exchange I am sure I would have left the field the bruised or bloodied loser."

"You flatter me, sir," Giovanni said graciously.

Megan was stunned. None of this made sense to her. She could no more than nod when Giovanni folded up Reed's page, stuffed it into his borrowed pockets, wished her good day, and left them.

"What was that all about?" she fairly exploded.

Reed shrugged, his eyes fastened to the door Giovanni had closed in his wake. "The settling of a disagreement."

"Reed! Names. Addresses? Who? And what have they to do with this?"

Brow furrowed, Reed crossed to the fireplace to study the charred remains of the page Giovanni had burned. Bending, he extracted a fragment of the writing that had survived intact. Crossing to the candle on the secretary, he gave the survivor no quarter. "If I asked you to do something, Megan, something I considered important to your safety and well-being, would you do it without question?"

"That would greatly depend on what you ask of me. I will not blindly promise."

His expression was unusually serious. "I would ask that you no longer frequent the company of Lord Frost and his sister Laura."

"Do you mean cut them off entirely?"

"I do."

"You would have me do this without benefit of an explanation?"

His brow wrinkled. "I realize I ask a great deal."

"I assume you saw fit to explain to Giovanni?"

"Correct."

Megan frowned. "I do not like to make uninformed decisions. Is the truth so shocking?"

Reed sighed. "I have no stomach for maligning another's character without firsthand proof of that person's wrongdoing. Giovanni was in danger, if the tales I have heard secondhand are true. I believe they are. You, too, are endangered by further contact with the Frosts, though perhaps not so perilously. I had hoped you would trust my judgment enough to agree to avoid them in future."

Megan considered his words. "All right. I agree. I will, on your recommendation, avoid the Frosts like the plague."

Chapter Eighteen

That evening Megan proved her intentions to adhere to Reed's request.

"Tomorrow, if the weather is fair, we must explore the ruins of the Roman fort that once guarded Hard Knott Pass," Tom said.

"Sounds vastly entertaining," Gussie agreed. "I suppose we should extend an invitation to the Frosts now that Reed means to abandon us."

"Not the Frosts," Megan said quickly. "I no longer care for their company, but Giovanni Giamarco might care to come along."

Gussie could not disguise her surprise. "Giovanni it is, then. Tom will send a note around to him this evening. Won't you Tom?"

Tom nodded. "By all means." He clapped Reed on the shoulder. "We will miss you, my good man, but as you can see, we are not to be stopped in our quest for the picturesque."

Reed laughed. "Nor should you stop. Indeed, I would like nothing better than to remain and assist in the quest."

Megan would have liked nothing better either.

Contrary to both their wishes, Reed departed early the following morning. He pulled Megan aside after breakfast for a private moment to kiss her good-bye on the cheek. For an awkward moment she wondered if he would buss her lips instead.

"Megan. About yesterday."

She knew what was coming. She had prepared herself for it. She had lain awake in her bed, staring at the ceiling for half the night composing in her mind what she supposed would be his careful explanation of what had happened between them. He would say something to the effect that his senses had run away with him, that she must not take the moment too much to heart. He would remind her that it had all been pretense of passion—a passion that was all too real to her. She had played and replayed their kisses in her mind—every unforgettable moment.

She did not want, could not stand, in fact, to hear his carefully worded explanation. She had, as a result, worked out exactly what to say.

"Oh, yes. The kisses," she said conversationally. "I had no opportunity to thank you."

"Thank me?" He sounded confused, but she could not risk looking at him. She would forget every carefully prepared word if she looked at him.

"Of course, thank you. Very instructional, those kisses. Most enlightening and more skillful than even I had imagined."

"But . . ."

She cut him off. "You were really quite convincing, I must confess."

"Wha—"

"Yes. Your pretense at passion for me. I almost began to believe it was real. Was I as convincing?"

She darted a glance his way. He looked a little dazed.

He frowned. "Were you . . . convincing? Unquestionably so."

"Good! I should hate to think you did not enjoy the experience as much as I did. I mean, if I did not know you as well as I do, I would surely fall head over heels in love with you on the sole basis of such kisses. They were remarkable. Really, quite remarkable!"

She was babbling. She knew she was babbling, but could no more stop it than she could stop his leaving. If not words flowing, it would be tears. "It is a good thing I do know you . . . that we are friends in every way. There can be no confusion between us when we have known one another for so long, right? I would not care to have confusion or misunderstanding between us, after all. Would you?" She forced every word to sound cheerful, steady, and convincing.

He was staring at her. She could feel his gaze following her, but could not, would not, turn to meet his gaze. Had she done so, she would most assuredly have given herself and her growing sorrow away to him.

"Megan." His voice was soft.

"Yes? What?" She sounded pitiful, so unsteady was her voice.

"I hate to be going. I hope to see you in London."

"Yes. London. It will be good to see you again before you leave for India . . . or is it, after all, the Americas?"

He frowned and raised his brows as if he had no answer ready for her.

She rushed on. "We must see the sights together: the Academy, the Townley Collection, the annual exhibit at the National Gallery. It will be great fun." She could say no more, else the tears that stung her eyes would have begun to flow.

Farewells and hugs all around and he held her very tight for a trifle longer than she might have expected before he leapt into the carriage and directed the driver. "Walk on."

Reed's carriage disappeared up the lane, wheels rattling, harness jingling, the horse's hoofbeats muffled on the dirt track. Megan stood listening until there was nothing more to hear.

"Oh, Gussie." Megan turned into her sister's shoulder with a moan. "What am I to do? He means to leave England. He means to leave me behind."

"Oh dear." Gussie offered a handkerchief though moisture threatened her own eyes. "Dear Megan. You have kissed him, haven't you? What a fool I have been to suggest such foolishness."

"No!" Megan said vehemently, dashing tears from her eyes. "Never blame yourself. I will cherish the memory for the rest of my life."

Gussie handed over her handkerchief and gave her shoulder a comforting squeeze. "Is there no hope for the two of you, then? None at all?"

Megan set her jaw. "No. Never has been. I am an extremely foolish girl to have believed otherwise."

It was in the main road leading out of Grasmere that Reed encountered Giovanni Giamarco, mounted, with a string of three saddle horses trotting behind him. Flinging down his window, Reed called to the driver to pause.

"Off to London, are you?" Giovanni shouted.

"Yes, and sorry to go."

Giovanni nudged his horse closer to the carriage window. "I am sorry to see the back of you." He spoke with a sincerity reflected in the crystal blue of his eyes. The two found themselves on new footing, based on the depth of understanding they shared. "You have yet to tell me if there is anything I can do to repay the debt of gratitude I feel I owe you."

"There is one thing," Reed replied thoughtfully.

"Anything!" Giovanni promised.

"Megan will be lonely for the remainder of her stay here, and in need of an escort when she goes on to London. Will you look after her?"

Giovanni sat up very straight in the saddle and looked Reed steadily in the eyes. "You may depend upon it. You honor me, sir. To entrust one so dear to you, to my care."

Chapter Nineteen

Once again, the well-laid landscape of Reed Talcott's life had been turned upon its head. Megan's kisses had moved a mountain of feeling within him. A river of yearning, too long damned up, had flooded the parched terrain of his heart. Reed did not like to leave the Lakes behind him. He did not like to leave Megan with so much unsettled and unsaid between them. He did not like to leave her in Giovanni Giamarco's care.

Feelings had sprouted within him, feelings he had never before allowed to seed. He had listened to Megan's garbled claim that there was nothing more to their kisses than pretense. Every feeling within heart and head rebelled. She could not mean what she had said. Could she? Did she feel for him none of the tumbled race of emotion, the yearning need and desire that now troubled him? Every word and glance she had shared with him seemed pregnant with new meaning. Every moment they had spent together at the Lakes bore reexamination.

As if he saw his life from a mountaintop, the hills, valleys, and rivers spreading, unclouded before him, he realized that his current financial disappointment was in fact a small thing compared to the great emotional desert that had been his. As rhythmically as the beat of the horses' hooves, as bruising as the ruts in the road, questions in an unending and unanswerable stream flowed through his milling mind. He had never before questioned the fact that Megan was his best friend. What was it they now shared? Love?

What little he knew of love, he had learned at Blythe Corner. Megan's family shared a warm, playful tenderness, that had, at times, almost overwhelmed him with jealousy. Why could he not witness such pleasant discourse, such gentle bantering within his own family?

In the last weary leg of his journey into London, with the mountains far behind him and the quiet with which he had so recently filled his ears lost in a medley of too many hooves and too many wheels on paved roads, Reed worked himself into a bit of a state, a temper most unusual. A blended rage of emotion possessed him: fear, anger, love, hatred. Overriding it all was the feeling that he had been betrayed by those who should have loved him most. Anguish tore at his heart, an anguish built from the lost potential of what might have been. It was in this state he arrived, late in the evening, upon his father's doorstep.

He was met at the door by Marsden, his father's butler, with the information that Lord Talcott was not at home to visitors.

Something inside of Reed snapped.

"I am not a visitor," he said tersely, pushing past Marsden. "I am Lord Talcott's son. You will not turn me away. Take my coat, have a footman see to the horses, and tell me at once where I may find my father. Upstairs, perhaps?" he guessed, his gaze fixed on the stairs where he had stood long ago, looking down on his father and mother as they tore asunder everything he knew to be good and true in an argument over a music teacher.

The sound of a woman's throaty laugh and the low rumble of a gentleman's reply from the dining room, not two yards from where he stood, turned his attention toward the double doors before which the butler positioned himself.

"His lordship is not to be disturbed." Marsden's voice

was hushed. "He asked specifically not to be interrupted—"

Ruthlessly, Reed thrust past him. The ledgers that held his pitiful life's story piled in one arm like a battering ram, he opened the door on a scene straight out of one of Hogarth's etchings of the *Rake's Progress*. His father, clad in no more than his shirt and a pair of gartered stockings, his wig askew, lolled on a comfortable chair drawn up before the dining table, on which reposed the remains of a sumptuous meal, four empty wine bottles, and a naked woman of voluptuous proportion.

The woman must have been a beauty once. There was still the fading bloom of it in the exaggerated hourglass of her figure, in the curling length of her hair and the gentle laugh with which she met the opening of the door. But the walnut shade of her tresses had a manufactured look and the milk white expanse of her thighs had begun to curdle. Her face, like that of a china doll, was aided and abetted in its claim to youth by heavy application of paint.

"Dear God! She's lying on the Spode!" breathed the butler.

Unfazed, either by the condition of the china, or the tarted-up trollop who lolled atop it, Reed, his goal clear, his mode unstoppable, slammed the ledgers onto the table. "I must ask you, sir," he demanded, "did you do this because you do not truly consider me your son—blood of your blood? Did you hope to leave another man's bastard, though he might wear your name, penniless?"

The woman on the table, heedless of the fearsome clatter of fine bone china against Waterford crystal, picked up the corner of the tablecloth as if it were a shawl, and covered the more blatant parts of her nakedness.

"What?" His father, like a phoenix from ashes, rose roaring from the chair. "What in blazes do you mean, bursting in on me like this without warning?"

"What warning did you give, sir, that my inheritance had all been spent on an indulgent manner of living that far exceeds your means?"

There fell a silence, thick as the pudding congealing on the sideboard.

The woman, who had thus far remained silent, further wrapped the tablecloth around her torso. "I believe this must be my cue for an exit, my dear," she said politely to Reed's father before jumping down from the table in a tinkling hail of fine crystal and now worthless china. With theatrical flair and a completely deaf ear for the havoc she wrought, she nonchalantly made her exit, dragging the tablecloth after her like a royal train—china, crystal, and plate crashing down in her wake.

Marsden leapt forward to capture in one hand a crystal goblet that teetered on the edge of the table. With the other he scooped up an unbroken gravy boat, before it sailed away on the surging tide of the tablecloth. His expression carefully devoid of emotion, he asked blandly, "Does madam require her carriage?"

"Madam does." The woman's voice echoed from the hallway. "Her clothes as well."

With an economy of movement, Marsden gathered together the scattered clothing and left the men. Father and son watched him go with equal expressions of wordless awe.

"Damn," Lord Talcott swore when the door closed gently on the last traces of his evening's entertainment. "You had better have a bloody good excuse for interrupting this evening's business. I have worked six months on the wooing of that woman."

Reed thumbed open one of the ledgers. "An expensive indulgence. More than four hundred and seventy-five pounds you had spent on her as of the middle of last month."

"As much as that?"

"Yes, and ill could you afford it."

"How ill?" Lord Talcott still stared at the door. His

voice rose in anger. "You had better bring me word that I've not two groats to rub together if you mean to interrupt me as you have done."

"I do."

Those two tersely uttered words won him attention.

"Do what?"

"Bring you word that you have not two groats to rub together."

"No, it's never as bad as all that."

"My mother's words exactly, sir, but I must disappoint you as much as I have disappointed her. You have no money."

"None?"

"None! As I've even less desire to inherit your debts as I've to inherit nothing, I have made arrangements to deal with the situation. There are papers here that require your immediate signature."

"It is *all* gone?"

"All of it but the five percents, a few bonds, and the properties."

His father blinked, his eyes glassy and blank. "It cannot be."

Reed marveled that his father could be so completely oblivious to the state of his fortune—or lack thereof. "It can and is. I have checked the figures thrice." He flung a page with rows of neat and irrefutable numbers in front of his father.

Lord Talcott fell silent, studying them. When his gaze rose from the bottom line his expression was haggard. "What was it you said when you first burst through the door?"

Reed had no desire to repeat what he had said. He could see by his father's demeanor that the harshness of their reality came as a shock. "I do not recall," he lied

His father had closed his eyes, his head lolled back upon a cushion, but his brow furrowed in concentration. "No, no, I have it now," he said, and eyes still closed he repeated, "Did I do this because I do not truly consider you, my son—blood of my blood?" His eyes opened to stare at Reed. "You think I did this on purpose? Out of spite?"

"The thought did cross my mind, sir, that you might prefer to spend every penny rather than leave it to a son you believe to be a byblow foisted off on you by an unfaithful wife."

His father closed his eyes again. "You are no bastard, Reed. Your resemblance to my father, your grandfather, who died before you were born, is too marked to deny. No, I did not pauper us by design. Ignorance and carelessness are my only excuses."

"Do you use the same excuse for your abandonment of your only son?"

Lord Talcott cleared his throat with gravelly anger. "Do you mean to send me into a seizure, boy?"

Reed considered holding tongue. He had already said and done far more than he had every dreamed himself capable of, but the words would not be stayed. "I have missed your presence throughout the great majority of my life, sir. I would not risk losing you entirely now that we do, on occasion, share words."

His father rose, drew on his breeches, and buttoned them as he crossed to the decanters on the sideboard. "I find myself desperately dry at the moment. Disaster does that to a man, you know." He poured amber liquid with shaking hand, crystal clinking erratically against crystal. The tremor was under control only when he had downed the shot in a single gulp. "Care for something? You can probably tell me how dear this cognac cost me, but I beg you will refrain."

"A brandy would be fine, sir." Reed took the proffered glass and sipped a liquid fire almost as searing as the truths he had come to deliver.

His father fortified himself with a second drink. "You mentioned something about arrangements, and my signature required?"

"Yes, sir." Reed licked his lips nervously. They tasted

of the French cognac they could no longer afford to indulge in. "Our only way out of this mess, as I see it, is to sell off all properties that do not provide income, along with all unnecessary but valuable assets, the monies therefrom to be invested in properties that will provide income."

"And you would sell?"

Reed read from a list he had prepared. "The country home in Devon. Rents received from the tenants are not promising. The hunting box in Surrey. The houses here in London. The apartments in Brighton and Bath."

"Rusticating, am I?"

"Yes. In addition, all of the horses and carriages but these must go." He extended a list. "All silver, paintings, rugs, furnishings, and china but these." He extended another list, saying wryly as he examined some of the china shards that littered the floor. "Minus the Spode of course."

"Of course." His father sighed. "What of the Keep?"

"The land thereabout has potential that must be more fully utilized, the north tower should be torn down and the roads repaired in trade for the building materials salvaged."

"And the servants? Some of them, like Marsden, have been in my employ their entire lives."

"Those affected by the sale of properties mentioned will need to be considered on a case by case basis, as well as those currently in attendance at the properties we mean to keep. The rest will have to be let go."

"Dear God! Your mother . . . ?"

"Has yet to be told."

"She will take it hard." He actually sounded as if he cared.

"I mean to sell off all of the plate from the Keep as well as the rugs, tapestries, and a good bit of the furniture."

"Dear God. She will come after me with a carving

knife. Tell me, will she think I have done this out of spite, just as you did?"

"I cannot claim to know the workings of my mother's mind, sir, other than to say she has had some small part in paupering us."

"Has she, by God? Do you refer to her dancing and music master, then? Have they been blackmailing her to hold their silence?"

"You knew?"

"I had my suspicions." He waved his half-empty glass at Reed as if to toast him. "You have just confirmed them."

He laughed when Reed uttered a sound expressing his regret. "Does she ever speak of me, your mother?"

Reed was surprised by the question. "On occasion, sir."

"And then only with loathing, I wager." His father tossed back the drink and let out a noise that sounded curiously like a sigh before he said in a softened voice, "I know you have little enough reason to confide in me, son, but have you ever been in love?"

"Yes, sir."

His father turned, surprised, his body swaying drunkenly with the suddenness of his movement. "True love? Not just carnal connection, but a deep and meaningful relationship? The kind that will not fade as age and beauty does, but might warm you through a lifetime?"

"Yes." Reed's voice was stronger. Megan's face rose instantly in his thoughts. She would warm him through a lifetime.

"Have you told the girl you love her?"

Reed was silent, unwilling to reveal so much of himself to this man who was little more than a stranger to him.

His father seemed to require no answer. "I was in love with her, you see."

Reed wondered who, among the scores of mistresses had usurped his mother's rightful place in his father's heart. "In love, sir, with whom?" he asked coolly, with little real desire to hear the answer.

"With your mother."

Reed was stunned, so stunned he dropped his glass. Dully, he looked down at the spilled liquor and broken bits. It ran through his mind that it was Waterford crystal and must now be struck from his list.

His father laughed bitterly. "Shocked you, have I? No, leave it," he protested as Reed bent to pick up the larger bits of glass "Marsden is waiting just outside the door with a broom to whisk away all damages as soon as we are done. You may depend upon it."

Reed left the glass. Crossing to the table, he drew out a chair and sank down into it. "I can depend on my memory, sir, for no evidence of this love you refer to."

"Evidence?" His father's voice was rough. "I left none. I was in love, but too full of pride to let it be known. You see, I was sure Clarissa Grant had married me for no other reason than my money."

"I have been informed it was a marriage of convenience."

"She told you that?" His father's eyes looked tired and very bloodshot.

"Yes, sir."

"I would that it had been. I was wrong. I did not find out *how* wrong until three years after I cast her, and you, from this house."

"I remember that day, sir."

"No doubt."

"You were saying, sir, that you were wrong?"

"Yes. It was in bedding a woman who had once been privy to your mother's confidences, that I discovered what a fool I had been." Lord Talcott set down his glass. With the flats of both hands he rubbed at his eyes, his attention focused on the past. "The woman I was rogering, I will not bore you with her name, found a wicked sort of humor in revealing to me all that had once been revealed to her in strictest confidence. According to her, your mother thought she might stir some spark of jealousy in taking a lover."

"Did it?"

"Of course it did. I was outraged. She hoped to make me abandon bad habits, you see."

"You did not."

"Of course not. By the time I realized I should have, it was too late. Much too late."

"Why too late?"

"Your mother's love for me had turned to disgust, even hatred."

"Ah."

"Yes. There is a fine line, you see, where passions are concerned. If you have found love, my boy, do not let it slip through your fingers as easily as your glass. It can be just as brittle, and no more mendable when smashed."

Chapter Twenty

His father's words stayed with him. Was there, Reed wondered, as fine a line between friendship and passion as divided love and hate? Strangely, it was in once again setting eyes on the Yat that all feeling with regard to Megan was brought into perspective. He leaned out of the open window of the carriage as it came in view of the familiar landmark, the wind in his face, dust blowing to the rear of the carriage like a rooster tail of white.

Here was the hill whose grandeur he had never fully recognized until he went away from it, just as he had not truly recognized the strength of his bond with Megan until he left it in the care of Giovanni Giamarco. He loved Megan! He had always loved her! It had taken distance, a fresh perspective, and a kiss to see the complete truth of the matter. He was in love and yet did not feel free to tell his beloved, to write to her—not until his future, miserable as it might be, was secure.

However, it was with a feeling of lightheartedness that he paused briefly at Blythe Cottage, that he might run inside, hug Megan's mother, and kiss her cheek.

"Goodness me, Reed!" Mrs. Breech exclaimed. "How lovely to see you. Are you only just now returned? Are Megan and Gussie faring well? Tell me more of this Italian, Giovanni, with whom Megan fills her letters. Do you have news?"

Her words, like the prick of a pin to the balloon of his happiness, left him flattened. "She writes of Giovanni, does she? Well, Megan has always been an admirable correspondent, has she not? I think it best she tell you all there is to say about Giovanni Giamarco. Regrettably, I cannot linger to chat. I have rather urgent business to attend to at the Keep."

"Nothing serious, is it, Reed?" Mrs. Breech was all concern. "Your parents, they are well?"

"Well enough, given the circumstances. No one is sick or dying, so in the grand scheme of things, I would have to say our troubles are not serious."

She gave him a strange look as he left her. Indeed, his leave-taking could not have been more abrupt, but away he rattled, up the last dreadful stretch of unrepaired road to Talcott Keep, his thoughts of Megan together with Giovanni bruising his spirit as much as the ruts in the road bruised his backside. The road pained him today as it had never succeeded in paining him before. Its every rut and pothole seemed calculated and vindictive, evidence of love turned sour. A tragic work of spite, he considered the disrepair.

There was tragedy, too, upon his arrival, in finding his mother closeted away with Monsieur Vincennes.

He did not burst in on her, as he had his father, but banging briskly upon the door, as he had never dared to in the past, saying, "Mother. I require an interview if you will be so good as to join me in the yellow drawing room at your earliest convenience. It is a matter of importance."

"But of course," her voice, unruffled, came from the other side of the door.

Her convenience, as it so happened, required the better part of an hour. Reed was left cooling his heels in the yellow drawing room contemplating the wisdom of having left Megan in Giovanni's care. He composed a list of the room's entire contents, with ticks beside the items he considered most valuable, and double ticks beside those that could be put up for sale.

"Reed." His mother arrived at last to greet him with

cool kisses and a wave of perfume. "How gratifying to a
mother that her son should exhibit so boisterously his
desire to speak with her on the instant of his return." She
couched her reprimand with eminent politeness and yet,
her words, no matter how mild, cut him. She ended the
remark with an unmistakable verbal jab. "How much
more gratifying if he should display a more mannerly
constraint."

"How do I find you, Mother?" Reed refused to rise to
her bait. The Pom was gone, he noticed. Fallen from
favor, he surmised. Did she love anyone or anything
with a sense of committment?

She frowned and turned her back on him, crossing to
the tall, narrow, arrow-slit window. "Sit down," she said.
"I have news, Reed, that you will not care to hear."

So closely did her statement echo the one forming on
his own tongue, that he was left speechless for a moment. "Bad news, Mother? Anything you have to tell me
cannot, I am quite certain, compare in magnitude to the
news I bring."

That got her attention. She turned to lean against the
arch, her gaze fixed on him. "Oh? Perhaps you should
tell me first then. You do not look happy. Did you not
enjoy your little holiday with the Breech girl?"

Again the blunted stab of her words.

"Every moment spent in Megan's company was a
pleasure," he said with conviction, "however, you are
correct in assuming me unhappy."

"Oh? What troubles you, Reed?" she encouraged in a
bored fashion.

"It is vastly unsettling to discover that I have not an
inheritance to look forward to."

"What?" She shot up from the wall, her eyes flashing.
"Does your father in any way dare to deny your right to
the claim?"

"He denies me nothing. There is nothing at this point
to deny, other than properties I will not be able to afford
and a mountain of debts to be paid."

Clearly shaken by what he had to say, she sought the nearest chair and sank into it. "You jest!" she suggested, as if in saying so it would be so.

"I wish our situation were, in any way, worthy of jest."

"This cannot be," she insisted. Her voice lacked conviction.

"It can and is. I have just returned from London. Father and I . . ."

"Your father knows of this before I have been informed?" Anger steadied her shaken resolve.

"There were papers that required his immediate signature."

"I see." She did not sound as if she saw at all. She did in fact sound outraged as she rose from the chair to pace the length of the room. "What have the two of you cooked up together to fix this mess?"

"As of yet, we have no fix, only stop-gap measures to halt the growing mountain of debt."

"What papers required your father's signature?"

"We are selling things, Mother, to meet the debts."

"Things? What things? Not my things. I will not suffer for your father's folly."

He handed her the same lists of properties, horses, carriages, and furnishings that he had shown his father.

She scanned them in silence before tossing them onto a fainting couch as if they contained personal insult. "This is outrageous! There must be some other solution! These are family heirlooms!" She seemed desperate for another solution. "Have you considered marriage, Reed? Surely you could . . ."

"Marry into money? As you did? How can you even open your mouth to wish your fate on me?"

"What would you have then? Poverty and Megan Breech? Do you think she can make you happy?"

"Yes, I do."

"Ha," she barked, crossing in her agitation to the window, where she peered through the narrow slit that looked out over the road that led to London. "I did once hope for happiness myself, but believe me, there is as much misery in love as ever there can be in money, if one loves the wrong person."

How often, Reed wondered, in the passing years had she stood there, watching and waiting for a love that had never opened its eyes to her and come chasing up the hill—a love in which she had long since given up. He understood, as never before, the depth of her anguish.

"Was my father the wrong person?" he dared to ask.

She whirled on him, her eyes flashing angrily, her voice pinched. "This has nothing to do with your father. Whatever gave you such a nonsensical idea?"

"I think you loved him. I think he loved you, too, but was blind to the truth of it."

"Nonsense!" she insisted vehemently, too vehemently, Reed thought. "But if you are foolish enough to marry Megan Breech, you could count on nothing but misery."

He laughed. "Then give me misery. I mean to marry her if I am left with anything at all to offer other than my undying affection."

She laughed. It was a strangely pinched, almost an hysterical sound. It brought tears to her eyes.

"Do not laugh," he snapped irritably.

She laughed harder.

He hated her in that moment as he had never allowed himself to hate her in the past. Turning swiftly on his heel, he stalked to the door.

"Bravo, Reed," she gasped, her amusement controlled before he could escape. "I had begun to believe you were too much your father's son ever to recognize the girl's . . ."

He whirled. "The girl's what, Mother? I warn you it had best not be a word against her. Not one word, as she may one day be your daughter-in-law."

She fell silent a moment, studying him. "I never intended to speak ill of her, Reed. I rather like Megan

Breech. It was the girl's infatuation for you I wondered if you had at last recognized."

"Infatuation with me?" He was confused.

"Yes." She laughed again, but unaccountably, her laughter turned to tears. "Has been for years, poor girl, and you completely oblivious to it."

Reed made offer of his handkerchief. She waved him away. "I had begun to fear you were too much like your father to notice the depths of her adoration."

"How did you know?"

"One has but to look at her. It is writ plain on her face, Reed. Whenever you step into the room she lights up like a candle. The wonder is *you* did not recognize it sooner. Tell me, was it out of some sort of misguided affection for Megan that you had that dreadful bronze made? The satyr. The one with her face on it?"

That stopped him cold. "You have seen the bronze?"

"Yes. So has Lady Burnham, more's the pity." She was laughing again, something wild in the sound.

"Lady Burnham? How in God's name has she seen the satyr?"

"Dreadful woman! She came to commiserate with me over her son's proposal to Megan."

"And you felt compelled to show her the bronze?"

Her chin rose abruptly. Her lips compressed into a severe line before she burst into the strangely hysterical laughter again. "No. In an effort to relieve her fears, I mentioned Megan's talent at watercolors. I took her to your study to examine the one you had so nicely framed while you were gone."

"Dear God!" Reed ran his hand nervously through his hair. "She saw the bronzes did she?"

"Yes. Well, one of them at any rate, before she fainted. Fell quite heavily, she did. Gave me such a fright, her head banging twice upon the floor as it did. I feared she was suffering an apoplectic fit and might give up the ghost right there. All the while Tidbit was sniffing at her face and barking loud enough to raise the dead di-

rectly in her ear. When she had been revived, and it was
no easy task, requiring both smelling salts and burnt
feathers, she took her leave, complaining the entire time
she was helped down the stairs about how dreadfully she
was suffering the headache—and no wonder with a knot
the size of a goose egg on her forehead—how strangely
deaf she was in the one ear and how shockingly improper the bronze was. She considered it an abomina-
tion, an affront to God, Harold, the church, and Megan's
family."

"And you, Mother? What did you think of it?"

"Well, I had no idea what she was talking about. So I
went back to your room and had a look. They are striking, Reed. I was most intrigued when I realized, upon
closer examination, that there was not one, but two
bronzes possessed of Megan's features. It occurred to me
then, that the figures looked rather like your work. Tell
me, Reed, why in God's name do you possess such likenesses of Miss Breech?"

Reed's hands roved over the bronze of Megan's look-
alike clasped in the arms of the satyr he should never
have drawn. He imagined Lady Burnham passed out in
the middle of his new Austrian rug, his mother waving
burning feathers beneath her nose. He chuckled dryly.
No need to worry about Harold Burnham's pursuit of
Megan anymore.

And yet, Harold never had concerned him. Giovanni
did. His gaze roved uneasily from the tapestry of Narcissus and Echo to the bronze in his hands. The disturbing
image of Megan, clasped in Giovanni Giamarco's arms
distracted him from all thought of Harold, distracted
him, too, from his goal, which was to decide how best to
invest his time and efforts that he might make a living.
He put down the bronze and shook away the troubling
idea that he should race at once to Megan's side. His direction must be clear before he went to her with a decla-
ration of his feelings. He meant to ask her to bind her

future to his. What that future might be, must be decided. What was he to do? What could he do? What had he done thus far with his life? He stared, unseeing, at his wall full of ordinance maps. He had pinned flags to the wall. He had pushed pencils and paintbrushes across countless pages. He had seen a little of the world. Was that all? Was there no more substance to him than that?

Life, as he knew it, would soon be swept away from him, pulled from his grasp piece by piece by bill collectors and creditors. He could not paint for his supper. As much as he enjoyed painting, as much talent as God had endowed him with, he lacked brilliance. He frowned, determined to find answers, not to wallow in self-pity and doubt.

What was it Megan had said? That the answers were generally right under one's nose, if seen from the right perspective. What were his choices? His talents? Surely his education and artistic skills counted for something. His gaze roved, searching out the promised answer.

The bronzes. Row after row of tiny women mocked him in their silent poses. The bronzes! A sculptor had thought enough of his sketches to create a pair of bronzes from them. There was always the chance the man might want to work from more of his drawings. Hope dawning, he wrenched open his sketchbooks, combing them page by page, one after another, for more sketches that might work as sculpture. But the sketches for Megan's bronze were quite singular in their beauty. Nothing quite like them graced the many pages of his sketchbooks. Megan's suggestion that his collection looked very much like a guidebook resurfacing, he made a pile of his better drawings and watercolors from his Tour.

To the group of sketches he attached a letter to a gentleman in London whose name appeared as publisher in several of the guidebooks that lined his shelves. Binding them together, he prepared them for posting.

There! That was a start. The idea was not lucrative

enough to make a living, but it was a beginning. What else did his education, his countless hours of rote memorization and recitation prepare him for? To what constructive end was his list-making and map-making suited?

Reed sat himself at the desk and wrote up a list of possibilities. It was a short list, a list that depressed him. He could not see himself engaging with any enthusiasm in any of the occupations he had written down. Anything, of course, was preferable to being hauled off to debtors' prison. His gaze roved the room. How stupid he had been, how blind—to go galavanting off to Europe, blithely throwing money away on bronze trinkets and tapestries he could in no way afford. He turned his back on the collection he no longer took joy in and walked to the arrow-slit window to look out over the visible bit of countryside. He felt a prisoner today, a prisoner in the landscape of his own ignorance.

There were no answers to be found outside the window, and while there seemed even fewer to be found within the walls of Talcott Keep, he turned to face his room again.

The maps on his wall offered no clear direction. Should he go to India? Perhaps look for a fresh start in America? Should he turn his back on England, his parents, and their money problems just as they had turned their backs on him throughout most of his childhood, too caught up in their own self-absorbed lives to notice how much he craved their attention, their love and affection?

Could he turn his back on Talcott Keep and Blythe Corner forever? Could he, in all fairness, ask so much of Megan? What a pompous, self-centered ass he had been to sit here, in his tower, assuming himself above the common cares of the world, pinning judgment and recrimination all over the map of other men's toil. What was it Megan had said that day at the quarry? "The picturesque is a luxury of the leisure class."

He no longer numbered among the leisure class. Far

from it. Time to decide by his actions his own worth. Out of habit, the comfortable square of his Claude glass filled his palm. He peered through the rose-colored square. The maps on his wall softly blurred pink. The problems he faced could not have been clearer. He could no longer frame his life with distance and an absence of emotion.

Like the water in a force fed by too much rain, anger and frustration welled within him. With an oath, he threw the folio of Claude glasses across the room. In a positive explosion of dislodged flags, it struck his pointlessly meticulous and involved map of England, lenses shattering, rose, umber, and ocher shards flying in all directions. With the violent intention of tearing down the well-flagged evidence of his absence of purpose, he crunched through the broken glass to grab the top edge of a map.

In the very instant that he did so, the Lake District caught his eye, the remaining colored flags indicating slate mines, copper mines, graphite and coal, the fat blue lines evidence of the growing system of water canals. In a flash something clicked in his brain with such perfect symmetry, such simple clarity, it stayed his hand midair. The writing was on the wall! Not pointless map pinning after all. Here was the answer! Under his very nose! Just as Megan had predicted.

Chapter Twenty-one

Megan viewed the Annual May Exhibition at the National Gallery, not in the company of Reed Talcott as she had hoped, but with Harold Burnham. Normally, she would have enjoyed the gallery no matter who accompanied her. The walls here were covered, four and more deep, floor to ceiling, in rows of paintings; gods and goddesses, prophets and portraits, landscapes and lapdogs.

She was not enjoying herself, however. Harold had, he told her, something of moment to discuss with her. Only now that they were together, he seemed reluctant to broach the matter. Megan dreaded it as well, for the only topic she could think that Harold might need to discuss with her was his proposal of marriage.

There was no end of potential springboards for their discussion. Everywhere, on every wall and in every alcove, there were depictions of lovers loving and kissers kissing. Fat cherubs kissed shapely, naked goddesses. Dark, half-naked men embraced fair, half-naked women. Young men stole kisses of young women in gardens, beneath mistletoe and beside haystacks. Judas, in the ultimate betrayal, kissed Christ. The painted expression of passions to which she had only recently been introduced, met her gaze everywhere she turned, reminding her of Reed, of wild, wet kisses and the sounds of rushing water. All around her were canvas-trapped views and vistas that brought to mind no one so much as Reed, from whom she had heard nothing. She focused for a moment on Harold's lips as he spoke. She tried to imagine kissing him with any sort of passion—tried and failed.

Was she enjoying herself, Harold asked. Did she not find the streets far too filthy and noisome? Was she not homesick so far from family, friends, and familiar faces?

"London is a noisy, smelly place," she agreed. "But what wonders! I never imagined a place so crowded and lively." She gestured toward her aunt, who strolled several paces in front of them flourishing her ivory-topped, ebony walking stick. Aunt Winifred had no real need of a walking stick, her stride was as vigorous, her balance as even as a much younger woman. She affected its use, she had told Megan, "because it lends a most distinguished air." Unobtrusively chaperoning, but for an occasional speaking rap of the aforementioned walking stick, she appeared to be with them for no other reason than to enjoy the paintings in the company of her best friend Mrs. Blaynay.

"Aunt Win has gone out of her way to make me feel welcome. She has introduced me to any number of her friends. Every day we receive a deluge of invitations. Fetes, soirees, dances, and teas. My head fairly whirls."

"I have heard you are to be seen often in the company of a handsome Italian."

"Oh? You must mean Giovanni. A wonderful fellow. I shall make a point of introducing you. Giovanni surprises me, you see. We met, quite casually, while I was at the Lakes. I had no idea at the time, nor did he make it clear, that he is the second son of a count. His father is a wealthy and influential man. I have been so informed by more than one well-born damsel who has tried to detach Mr. Giamarco from my arm when he has been kind enough to offer himself as escort. He has surprised me, too, Harold, in behaving the complete and proper gentleman in every way. He struck me, you see, when first we did meet, as too passionate a fellow."

"Too passionate?"

"Yes, as his countrymen are often characterized. I believed him undependable where ladies were concerned."

"Undependable? In what way undependable?"

"Well, to put it quite frankly, I thought he bestowed his affections without discrimination."

"No discrimination. Undependable. Too passionate, and yet you are seen with him everywhere."

"Yes." She saw nothing strange in it. "He has proven me wrong on every front. You will like him immensely. I am sure of it. He and Reed did not like one another at all at first, but they have become the best of friends."

"Reed. Have you spoken to Reed of late?" Harold wore a troubled look when he asked. His expression so perfectly matched Megan's own mood that she did not stop to think why Harold should find mention of Reed troubling.

"No. I have not seen or heard from him, though I have looked for him at every gathering. He is supposed to be in London soon. He will regret having missed our outing today. He expressed a particular desire to see the National Gallery when last we spoke."

"Did he?" Harold cleared his throat.

"Yes. There is nothing so delightful to a painter as examining other people's paintings, and there are landscapes Reed would love to see. They adhere precisely to the romantic tenets he believes in so fervently."

"Romantic tenets? Yes, well. I do not know much about that. I know next to nothing about painters and paintings." He paused before a depiction of a nude Venus. "Tell me, do artists often work from models?"

Her eyes were still occupied by a landscape that reminded her of the Lakes. "But of course. Some landscape artists recreate entire scenes in miniature in their studios, using pebbles to represent boulders and twigs as trees."

He gestured toward the nude Venus. "What about people? Did a real young lady pose for that?"

She studied the Venus. "I would say yes, based on the

very realism of her form. There is nothing better for the artist than to work from reality."

"Uhm, have you, I hesitate to ask, have you ever . . . posed . . . for Reed?"

"Oh yes," she answered without hesitation. "Many times."

His startled gaze no longer centered on the Venus, but on her, brows raised.

"Not like that of course." She gestured toward the canvas.

"No?"

"No!"

"Never?"

"Do you mean to suggest you think I would have posed in the nude?" She blushed.

He was staring at her in a disturbingly searching manner, as if imagining her without her clothes on. She had never suffered such an insulting perusal before. It left her itching with the desire to slap him.

"Really, Harold, I am surprised at you."

"I have had a letter from my mother."

"Oh?" She frowned. "What have letters from your mother to do with our current topic?"

"She was most distressed."

"Why? Does *she* think I have posed nude for Reed?" She smiled at the ludicrous idea.

He was not smiling. "She thinks you are shameless."

"What?" Her voice rose loudly enough to echo in the stillness of the gallery. Aunt Winifred's lorgnette raised in their direction. Megan lowered her voice. "Whatever gave your mother such a frightful notice of my sense of propriety?"

"She writes of a bronze that she has seen at Talcott Keep. She claims it can be no one other than you."

"Oh dear!" Megan covered her face with her hands, laughing.

Aunt Winifred's stick thumped irritably. She laughed even harder.

"From your reaction, I hazard to guess you are familiar with the bronze?"

"Yes." She choked back her amusement. "Well, yes. I know the bronze. And while the face is mine, the rest of it is culled from Reed's imagination."

Her words did not have the desired calming effect.

"Reed sees you that way?"

"Well . . ." She studied the question as she studied again the Venus. "He did not . . . at the time. The sculptor was to blame."

"The sculptor? Has *he* seen you in the altogether?"

His words triggered another fit of laughter from Megan, the noise of which spurred an absolute tattoo of censorious thumps from Aunt Win's stick

Megan stifled her amusement. "Of course not. I have never been to Italy."

"Italy? What has Italy to do with anything? I will not be distracted from the matter, Megan. Mother says you are attacked by a bronze man who is half goat."

"True," Megan said with a nonchalance that seemed to further provoke Harold's concern.

"Is he naked?"

"Not precisely, Harold. As a satyr he is depicted with hair for breeches."

"Sounds disgusting."

"Not disgusting in the least. It is art and mythology and though it would take a great deal of effort to explain, it is all very innocent."

"Your definition of innocent would appear to be far removed from mine. More than half of the paintings in this display do not fit my definition of decent."

"Really, Harold. I had no idea you devoted so much thought to indecency."

"I wonder if you have given much thought to my proposal?" He caught her completely off guard with the question.

"Your proposal? But of course. I have given it a great deal of thought. Why? I . . . Is there some connection be-

tween your proposal and Reed's bronze?" It occurred to
her he meant to cry off regardless of her explanations.

"I have given my feelings for you a great deal of
thought," he said.

"And have you had a change of heart?" The idea left
her relieved. She did not want to become Mrs. Harold
Burnham. Never had really. Strange, but she was, in a
way, disappointed as well. To have lost a man's affections, no matter how little she valued them, was a loss.
She could not deny it.

His gaze strayed from her face to the Venus and back
again. "Our interests would appear to be of a vastly di-
vergent nature."

"They are," she agreed. "And bound to be a source of
unhappiness between us. Perhaps it is best if we mutually agree that we do not suit, Harold."

"Yes," he agree. "Perhaps it is best."

It was odd, Reed thought, how it all came together before scattering, like a seedpod in the wind. Wagonload
after wagonload it arrived at Christie's Auction House:
furniture, rugs, china, silver, and artwork—from the
Keep, the country home, the town houses and hunting
boxes. The combined accumulation of carelessly acquired riches were all gathered together under one roof.

Christie's had, in the past few hectic, rainy days,
begun to feel like a transitory sort of home to him. The
smell here was even a bit like home if he closed his
eyes—all beeswax and polish. Everything that came in
Christie's door was given a fresh shine. And, for the moment, front to back, floor to ceiling, the rooms were
completely packed with what had once been home.

The staff at the auction house had become temporary
housekeepers to him. Soft-voiced and thorough, they
were not in the least inclined to sentimentality or
dawdling and had, with businesslike efficiency, led each
of the Talcotts through the most grueling few days Reed
had ever experienced. Together they had carefully exam-

ined, assessed, tagged and cataloged hundreds of items from the Talcott estate. As a result, he knew each of the attendants, sales clerks, and pricing experts by name. The staff in turn knew a great deal more of Talcotts than their name.

Discreet, polite, and respectful as they remained, they had to realize, every last one of them, how dire was the Talcott's current need for liquid assets that they would dispose of so many things at one time. Pounds and pence, every employee in the place began to formulate a picture of just what the Talcotts were worth. It was a considerable sum. Enough, Reed figured, to clear all debts and begin to establish a promising future for Talcotts to come.

Perhaps the most intimate detail of all, the Christie's staff knew that Lord and Lady Talcott, when they arrived, came in separate carriages and generally at different times of the day. When their paths, by happenstance did cross, the two did not acknowledge one another in any way.

"I have come to assist in cataloging the wine." Lord Talcott informed Reed halfway through the second day of pricing.

Reed looked up from a case of gold, silver, and ormulu snuffboxes. "John, will you give us a moment?"

"Certainly, sir." The clerk who assisted him promptly took himself off.

"How did the horses do at Tats?" Reed asked. His father looked exhausted.

"Good God, my boy!" With a heartfelt sigh Lord Talcott sank heavily into John Jones's abandoned chair. "Toughest thing about this whole business, selling my hunters. Foster and Blue Boy are safe, Buckingham has them. He is a knowing one with horses. The bays and the dapple gray have gone to good homes as well. But Old Foster looked confused when he was led away by a complete stranger and I came very close to knocking down the young buck who dared to suggest he meant to bob tails on both Great Day and Tassle! Can you imagine Tassle without that sleek, black broom of his?"

"I am impressed, sir, by your restraint."

"You have not heard the half of it," his father crowed. "Told the clothhead he must do as he saw fit, but that he risked throwing both of the animals completely off their stride in whacking off their tails. I take some pleasure in the fact that he payed through the teeth for both of them. The bidding was quite stiff. You can congratulate yourself on having a father who knows his horseflesh. The returns were gratifying"—he sighed again—"if difficult to bear."

"I am pleased to hear it! We shall need every penny. Word is out. Bill collectors hounded me all the way into the building today."

"I know, I know. They were camped out on my very doorstep this morning. But never fear. They shall all be paid in the end. My hunting boxes have been snapped up. Word arrived yesterday that an offer has been made for the property in Mayfair and closing papers are on their way from Bath."

"In a more positive vein"—Reed found it difficult to contain his excitement—"there is a slate quarry in the Coniston Fells, another near Kirkby, on which I am negotiating. In addition, our agent in Kent has located a promising property—an orchard—apples, pears, also black currents, raspberry, and loganberry bushes. The house is in disrepair. We will want to add on or tear it down and rebuild, but it is close to the proposed canal improvements, as we had discussed. He mentions hop vines have recently been staked and that they grow very well in the area. What do you know about the growing of hops?"

"Hops, you say? Not a blessed thing other than that they are required to make ale. The trick is to hire someone who does know." Beaming, Lord Talcott clapped Reed on the shoulder with pleasure. "Nothing ventured, nothing gained, eh? Why not give it a go?"

Strange, Reed thought, that he felt closer to his father now, in the middle of this fiasco, than he ever had when things were going well. "We do move merrily along with this business, don't we, sir?" he said.

Again his father clapped him companionably on the shoulder. "We have stepped out of the ordinary and into the extraordinary, my boy, and very invigorating I find it. High time and no sense dawdling, eh? Now, where is the wine kept? They have been careful not to stir the sediment have they not?"

"They have been very careful, sir, very helpful. The wine is this way."

As they set off, a woman's voice echoed from the room behind them.

Lord Talcott picked up the pace. "Your mother, Lord bless her," he said a trifle breathlessly. "She will not care to set eyes on me."

"The two of you will have to face one another eventually," Reed said, falling behind, refusing to be rushed.

Lord Talcott continued to advance rather more briskly than was called for. His voice carried in a muffled manner over his shoulder. "As you say, but perhaps it is best arranged when this nasty auction is over with. Lady Talcott cannot be in the most congenial of moods at the prospect of losing so much of her finery. I know I am not."

Reed settled his father with a clerk named Phillips in a room stacked with the contents of three emptied wine cellars and headed back through the viewing rooms in search of his mother. He walked swiftly, his eyes glazed a little to blur the sight of so much that was Talcott on every side of him. It would not do to look at the sale items too keenly.

He paused in the room where his landscapes were hung, unable to blindly pass the beloved views that would soon hang on other men's walls. A weight descended on his chest whenever he stood still long enough to regard his treasures. He would have liked to claim it was the weight of promise and not regret that pressed in on him, but though his future hung here, its potential suspended for the moment in these treasures from his past, he could not help but mourn the loss.

Jaw set, he put the room behind him. He was not the only one who suffered. His mother and father met the challenge with the bravest of fronts. Reed had never known his mother to work so diligently, even bravely. She had resorted not to handkerchiefs of histrionics in the disposition of her china and silver once it was made clear to her that debtors' prison or the Colonies were her only other options.

She came today to catalog her jewelry. Meeting Gerald Smythe, the pricing expert for jewelry, on his way to her side, he discreetly recommended, "An idea, Mr. Smythe! I wonder if you would be so kind as to present the jewelry for my mother's examination first in paper form in detailed description with values assessed, then, the jewels themselves, so that she is not compelled to look at her lost baubles overmuch."

"I understand entirely," Smythe agreed. "It shall be just as you have described."

"I understand your father is here?" his mother said tartly when he joined her. Her manner was unusually stiff. "Does he mean to avoid me?" she asked.

"Yes. He thought it best due to his uneven temper. He has just come from the sale at Tattersall's."

"His hunters. That must have hurt." There was the faintest trace of sympathy in her voice. "Did he get a decent price for the beasts?"

"He said it went as well as could be hoped."

She wore a glassy, stunned look more often than not these days. "There is some consolation in that, I suppose. Tell me again, Reed, about this connection you have made between canals and your proposed investment in slate quarries, coppice wood, and fruit trees. I would be clear in my mind why I am giving up my jewelry."

Reed patiently explained for perhaps the fifth time. "Water is the key, Mother."

"Water? You have said something about the water to me before, have you not?"

"Yes, no matter. This is all a trifle overwhelming, is it not?"

"That is a masterful understatement," she said softly, with a trace of her normal bite.

"Yes, well, via canal, anything may be more easily transported; stone, wood, fruit. With London growing at a great rate here in the south and Birmingham and Manchester booming in the north there will be a growing need for building materials, charcoal, and food. We mean to provide them, hopefully in great enough quantity that the Talcott fortune will begin to rebuild itself."

"And what does Megan Breech say to your plans, Reed?"

"I have no idea. I have yet to tell her."

"Well, get on with it, get on with it." She waved her hands briskly, though Reed had no idea whether she spoke to him or Mr. Smythe, who entered the room at that moment, bearing a large stack of velvet boxes.

Chapter Twenty-two

It was time, Reed decided, as his mother suggested, to talk to Megan—to tell her what plans he had laid for his future, a future he hoped she would share. He set out, therefore, on foot, in the misting rain, the half-dozen or so blocks it would take him to stroll to Megan's Aunt Winifred's town house on the east edge of Mayfair. He knew the address well enough. Twice he had walked the street, twice decided to wait to talk to Megan. What he was waiting for, he could not quite put a finger on. That he would know when he was ready—of that he was certain.

And now, despite the gathering darkness, the rain, and the carriage that splashed him with muddy water in cutting the corner too tight on Albemarle Street, he felt prepared to explain his plans, his changed future, his change of heart.

It was Giovanni Giamarco who stopped him. He was standing on the doorstep at number 21 when Reed rounded the corner, looking, as he had always looked, handsome and fit. The butler who answered his knock opened the door wide for him without hesitation, as if he came there often, smiling, bowing, and taking his umbrella and the large bouquet of flowers that were no doubt intended for Megan. Following his flowers over the threshold, Giovanni doffed his hat. The door closed behind him.

The sight slowed Reed. The door closing stopped his progress entirely. Could it be Giovanni paid serious court to Megan? Could it be his attentions where even more welcome than Reed might have assumed? Giovanni would, after all, be far more suitable a suitor at this point than he, would he not? He had far more to offer Megan.

Reed stood in the street, shifting from one foot to the other, wondering. There was a light in the window of what must be the sitting room at number 21. The figure of a woman was suddenly silhouetted against the lace curtain, rising to greet her guest, her figure too indistinct to determine if it was Megan or her aunt. There came the sound of muffled laughter through windows almost completely closed against the rain. Knowing he had little news with which to amuse anyone, Reed lost all desire to expose himself and his problems, even to his dearest friend. He turned his back once again on number 21 Bruton Place and walked away.

Aunt Win rose, trailing needlework on a hoop when Giovanni, his wildly curling hair glistening with rain, was shown into the sitting room. Megan did not rise, too immersed in the small type of an ad in the *Times*.

It was an ad for an auction to be held at Christie's, an ad so amazing she did not look up when Giovanni greeted her with a pleasant good day.

"Is it a good day?" she asked negligently. "It has done nothing but rain."

Unperturbed, Giovanni crossed the room to drop a spattered copy of *The Post* onto the table at her elbow. "You have seen it, then?"

Megan glanced up with a frown. He sounded all too cheerful. "The listing. Yes. It surprised me completely. Disastrous bit of news."

"Disastrous?" He sank down beside her with a smile, undeniable mischief in his dark eyes, raindrops glistening in his eyelashes. "You deem it disastrous then?"

That he could be so callous as to suggest otherwise

disappointed her. "Do you belittle our dear friend's misfortune?"

"Misfortune? Is marriage a misfortune? Is that why you will not agree to return to Italy with me?"

"Marriage?" Megan was confused. "Who is to be married?"

Aunt Winifred looked up sharply from her stitching. "I was not aware you had asked Megan to return with you to Italy, Mr. Giamarco."

"No?" Giovanni shrugged broadly, reminding Megan of Reed. "No great wonder. She refuses to take my marriage offer seriously."

"You have yet to answer my question." Megan snapped up the folded paper. "Is someone we know soon to be married?"

"It will not be you, my love," her aunt scolded, "if you make a habit of turning down every promising young man who offers for you."

"Aunt Win!" Megan hoped to stop her from saying any more. Her aunt had been gently but ceaselessly chiding her over the lost opportunity with Harold Burnham. She had once declared him a bore, but now that Megan had refused him she kept referring to him as "that promising young man."

"Turning down offers are you?" Giovanni asked, all interest. "What scoundrel, *cara*, dares to try to sway your affections from me?"

"My one-time suitor may be called many things, Giovanni, but scoundrel is not one of them," Megan said firmly.

"But who is he? I will call him out if he offends you with unwanted attentions."

"Ready to fight a duel over my niece, are you, Mr. Giamarco?" Winifred laughed. "What a droll notion. No, that will not do, sir, for he is a very promising young man of both title and wealth whom Megan has known since she was a little girl."

"What?" Giovanni looked surprised. "Has Reed Talcott bent knee to you then?"

"Talcott?" His response confused her aunt. "I thought his name was Burnham, Megan. Am I mistaken?"

"No. You are not mistaken, Mr. Giamarco is. Reed Talcott has not proposed, Harold Burnham has."

"I do not know this Burnham," Giovanni complained.

"And I do not know Reed Talcott," Winifred said tartly.

"No. Neither of you have ever been introduced to the parties in question," Megan said.

"Nor are you likely to be," Winifred said briskly. "Now that my niece has refused him."

Megan grabbed up the folded paper that had been thrown on the table at her elbow, in a bit of a pet. "Now that we have determined that I am not to be married to either of the gentlemen in question, I return to my initial query. Who is to be married?"

"Our Miss Frost." Giovanni pointed to the listing.

"Who?" Aunt Win asked.

"*Our* Miss Frost?" Megan objected. "She was never *my* Miss Frost in any way."

"Who is this Miss Frost?" Win asked again.

"She means to marry some poor fellow named Dunlevey," Giovanni said. "An earl, no less."

"Who? Who did you say means to marry Dunlevey?" Aunt Win had begun to sound like an owl.

Megan sent Giovanni a warning look. "Her name is Laura Frost. Related to the Earl of Banning. Her uncle, if I am not mistaken. A beautiful and rather calculating young woman I met at the Lakes."

"A fortune hunter is she?" Win stabbed at her needlepoint.

"However did you know that?" Megan was surprised by her aunt's inexplicable accuracy.

"Well, Lord Dunlevey cannot be a day less than sixty, and not in the best of health last I heard. And Banning is well known to have a pack of wastrels and hangers-on as nieces and nevvies."

Giovanni nodded, his expression gone dark and sad. "That is our Miss Frost all right, giving herself to a marriage that will soon leave her a wealthy widow."

Aunt Win shuddered. "Sounds a dreadful, grasping creature."

"Yes. And deadly charming," Giovanni agreed briskly. "It might be my misfortune to be listed on that page had it not been for Reed Talcott."

"Reed Talcott?" Megan and her aunt spoke in unison.

"The same Reed Talcott you thought had made Megan a proposal?" Win asked.

Megan fell silent. "The duel," she said abruptly.

"Duel? We are no longer talking about the duel my dear," her aunt said.

Oh, but they were, Megan thought. The paper and pen duel played through her mind.

Giovanni nodded. "The duel. Reed knew she was after my money. In the pages he wrote to me, he kindly revealed what little he knew of Miss Frost's rather sordid history. I have since discovered there is a great deal more to it. As a result, I am forever indebted to your friend Reed. His quick thinking and kindness have rescued me and my family from untold embarrassments. I do not know how I shall ever repay him."

"Has this Reed fellow been engaging in duels, then, Megan? Highly unsuitable behavior in this day and age. I am sure you must agree, Mr. Giamarco."

"How can I agree, without sounding the complete hypocrite?" Giovanni softened his response with a blinding smile. "It was I, after all, convinced him to engage in it in the first place."

Megan sat still a moment, absorbing the truth. So much more of what Reed had said that day made sense to her. All the pieces fell together. Her gaze settled on the ad she had been perusing—the shocking ad for Christie's, in which a number of very familiar watercolor landscapes and Italian bronzes were being offered up for sale. "You spoke of a feeling of indebtedness to Reed, Giovanni." She handed him the paper. "Perhaps you could begin to repay him, by bidding on a landscape or two at Christie's."

"What's this?" He took the paper and scanned the ad.

"Reed," she said.

"He is in financial trouble?" he surmised.

"Yes, and his situation must be dire indeed if he means to part with both the watercolors and the bronzes."

"They are dear to him?"

"Dearer than anything," she said bleakly, unable to imagine why Reed had not thought to come and tell her anything of his troubles.

Chapter Twenty-three

It was raining again on the day that Giovanni, Megan, her Aunt Win and Mrs. Blaynay set out for Christie's auction rooms. Pall Mall, when they reached it, was thick with restless horses, rain-slick carriages, and the shining black domes of drenched umbrellas. Pensively, Megan peered through fogged carriage windows at a colonnade-bracketed entrance and an expanse of rain-dotted plate glass. The carriage tipped and swayed as first Giovanni stepped down and then her aunt and Mrs. Blaynay.

The sway of the carriage added to the uneasy feeling in the pit of Megan's stomach. Here she would see Reed, at a time and place he might prefer not to be seen.

"Your turn." Giovanni leaned into the carriage, his gloved hand extended, ready to transport her as dryly as possible to Christie's door. "You look worried, *cara*."

"Do I?"

"*Sì*. There is a line forming between your brows. I am not used to seeing it there. Tell Giovanni, what is wrong?"

She sighed and forced a smile. His words stirred her memory of another rainy day not so long past and similar words said. "It is the rain—the stench of the city—the crowds," she lied. "I have just been wishing myself back in the quiet sunshine and beauty of the Lakes." That was true enough.

She took his hand, stepped carefully onto the carriage

step, and with her skirts gathered made a leap to clear
the litter-choked gutter.

Giovanni secured her elbow as she landed safely on
the pavement under cover of the umbrella he held high.
"I could take you, *cara*, if you would only let me, to see
the noble peaks of the Apennines topped with snow—
purple in the clearness of a sky so blue it makes your
eyes hurt. I could take you to walk in my mother's garden, a sunny place of fountains and labyrinths, smelling
sweetly of oranges, lemons, and cedar."

She stopped him, there in the street, with the doorman
holding wide the door to Christie's and her aunt and
Mrs. Blaynay shedding coats just inside and surely wondering what delayed her progress in the rain. "Are you
sincere when you say pretty things to me?" She had to
ask.

"Things, *cara*?" He looked at her with what she
thought must be a carefully cultivated expression of innocence. She was more than a little entranced by Giovanni Giamarco, darkly handsome, doe-eyed, and
appealing, his focus on her complete. He seemed to
known exactly what to say in order to please. And yet
she had no real desire to be bewitched by him. She had,
in fact, begun to think that a great deal of her appeal was
in her resistance to his charm.

"You say such pretty things, my friend, but I warn
you, do not play too loosely with my affections. You see,
I just might begin to believe you."

He smiled, mischief dancing in the enchanting depths
of soot-lashed eyes. "You give my heart wings to say
such a thing, Megan. Does this mean that at last you give
up all hope in our friend Reed?"

She blushed. "Is it so very obvious? My feelings for
him?"

Her aunt's walking stick thumped imperiously from
the doorway, reminding her of the impropriety of standing so long in the street speaking privately to a gentleman.

Giovanni paid the summons of the stick no mind.

"You forget," he said softly, "I saw the way you kissed him at the waterfall." His smile widened, his expression godlike and beautiful and yet not so loved as it might have been. "You pine for him," he said with certainty. "I see it in your eyes, *cara*, when you think no one notices."

For an instant she felt like throwing herself against his broad chest to weep. There was a level of inner beauty, of profound sensitivity in Giovanni, an awareness and understanding she had never expected to discover so handsomely packaged. But he was reaching up to collapse the umbrella and again Aunt Win tapped impatiently her walking stick. Megan could not throw herself at a river god without unwanted entanglement.

"Come," Giovanni said with bracing vigor, nodding her toward the still unctuously waiting doorman. "We will see what good we can do for our good friend Reed."

There was, Megan decided, a sense of urgency within the walls of Christie's that matched her mood.

It was on the top floor of the building that the auctions were conducted. To reach the bidding room, one had to pass first the front counters, where people brought in their treasures to be valued, then mount the stairs, footsteps echoing, following and being followed by a steady stream of people, also bent on reaching either the viewing or the auction rooms. Everywhere they turned, to her surprise, people were wishing Giovanni good day, tipping their hats to him, fluttering fans.

"*Merci beaucoup* for the tip," a gentleman with a French accent said sotto voce to Giovanni as he passed them.

"You have seen something you like?" Giovanni lowered his voice in an equally conspiratorial manner.

"There is a French commode I have my heart set on," the fellow admitted with a wink, "and so much more to be seen. I will not stop to chat."

Megan tugged on Giovanni's sleeve when he was gone. "Is this your doing?"

"What?"

"These people? This crowd? Your debt to Reed repaid, perhaps?"

Giovanni winked at her. "Something like that."

She was amazed. As another of those who viewed the antiques tipped his hat, she murmured, "What a lovely man you are, Giovanni."

He smiled at her, his expression so enchanting that any number of women nearby took notice and set to whispering behind their fans. "So I have been telling you all along," he said archly. "Will you not change your mind, signorina, and sail away with me to Italy when I depart for home next month?"

Megan smiled. For the first time since Giovanni had asked her, she seriously pictured what it would be like to travel to Italy as the wife of the handsome and thoughtful Mr. Giamarco. There was a sense of urgency to her thoughts. The time in which she might agree to such a picture was short.

There was a matching sense of urgency in the viewing rooms. Here, paintings and tapestries had been hung, rugs unrolled, furniture, and objets d'art beautifully arranged and displayed, with an oddly insensible juxtaposition and the omnipresent lot numbers to remind one that the arrangement of each room was a fleeting thing. These were temporary gatherings of a number of beautiful objects in one place before they were carried away by a host of new owners. The press of the crowd soon separated them from her Aunt Win, who had proclaimed her intention to immediately seek out the china to be auctioned.

Megan was in no hurry. In a swimming sort of daze she wandered the viewing rooms. At more than one point, she clutched Giovanni's arm for support. Everywhere she turned she recognized plunder from the Keep: russet-hued rugs, furniture, artwork, and bric-a-brac.

"Lady Talcott's silver," she said sadly. Carefully tagged and numbered, the glittering silver looked all wrong spread about on a sideboard rather than in neat rank and file in the butler's pantry at Talcott Keep.

"You are certain?" Giovanni asked.

"Yes. There is no mistaking that centerpiece. I have always admired it enormously."

"So, it is not just Reed who is forced to sell his possessions," Giovanni said.

"No. This is dreadful. You see before you the treasures of Talcott Keep. I feel as if I have come to walk about on a dear friend's grave when no one ever bothered to tell me there had been a funeral."

Hardest to bear was the sight of Reed's personal treasures: his collection of bronzes, his landscapes, the stunning tapestry of Narcissus and Echo.

"See. It is you." Megan pointed out the Narcissus who looked so very much like Giovanni. She choked on the words when she said, "It is the most beautiful tapestry . . ."

"But who is this?" Giovanni indicated the fading figure of Echo. "I have no one to pine for me so faithfully."

"Do you want such a transparent creature?"

"There is something very seductive, I think, in a creature so devoted," he said.

Megan smiled at him. "Would that Narcissus had only noticed that seduction before Echo had all but disappeared," she said, wistfully touching the tapestry for what she was sure must be the last time. "Come," she said. "Let us look at the bronzes. There are two I would be sure are not to be sold."

The lovely little family of bronze women, soon to be orphaned from one another, had collected a crowd of interested onlookers. A great many were jotting down lot numbers.

"What heartbreak it must be to part with these," Giovanni said softly. "They are marvelous!" He examined them carefully, one by one.

Megan examined the collection with even more appreciation than Giovanni. To her profound relief, two from the collection were notable for their absence. The bronzes of passion personified, the lovers and the satyr pairing, were not to be sold.

"Nutmeg! Is it you?" It was Reed who quietly addressed her, Reed, looking strained and awkward, bravely putting on his best face, his voice cool, collected, and as gentlemanly as always.

"Reed, how good it is to see you!" Giovanni turned from his examination of the collection and with theatrical Italian passion used Reed's extended hand as a lever to draw him into a back pounding embrace with robust kisses on each cheek.

Reed's subsequent palming of Megan's hand and his chaste peck on her cheek seemed disappointingly understated.

"How are you, Megan? I did not expect to see you here today!" He spoke with a formality to which she was wholly unaccustomed.

"I can well imagine you did not," she said with contained heat. "You did not, after all, extend an invitation to me. Perhaps you would have preferred I did not come."

He made a face. For a fleeting instant his pain in the day's proceedings was evident. "I am sorry, Megan."

"I am sorry, too." She gestured awkwardly toward the bronzes. "To see all of these things"—her voice faltered—"your mother's silver, the landscapes . . ."

"I know."

"Why did you not tell me?" she asked very low. "I thought you could tell me anything."

He exhaled heavily, his gaze darting through the crowd as if he sought an escape from her question. "Devilishly difficult, don't you see? Things have been happening rather fast, Megan." He spoke with a politeness, almost an uneasiness, as if she were, in Giovanni's company, a little-known acquaintance whom he had forgotten how to address. "I was not sure exactly what our circumstances were until the day before I left the Lakes."

"You knew and did not say a word?"

"Right." He would not look her in the eye. "I thought it prudent to inform my parents before anyone else."

"Of course." She implied understanding when she did not understand at all. That he had cut himself off from her in this, the most trying time of his life, wounded her deeply. The distance between them had never seemed so great. "Have you been in London long?" Her tone echoed his: awkward, distant, and polite, the nature of exchanges between strangers, not dear friends.

"How long?" It was another question he would rather not have been dealt. She could read it in his eyes. "Long enough to make arrangements for today. Too long not to have contacted you, I know, but I hope you will understand, there was a great deal of difficult decision-making to be done and I have been at a bit of a loss as to what to say to anyone. There is limited potential in responding to the expected how-do-you-dos with well enough other than that I have no money and am forced to sell everything I have ever possessed of any value." He presented the tragedy of his dilemma as if it were of no great moment. Laughing awkwardly, his glances uneasy, his hands spoke with greater emotional eloquence than his tongue, touching first upon his forehead, then his mouth, and finally settling themselves in hugging his own shoulders.

His jovial approach won a chuckle from Giovanni.

Megan could not laugh. "We would have found something to say to one another," she said, her pain undisguised. "We have always managed in the past."

"Yes." He frowned, fingering his neckcloth as if it were too tight. He looked about the room again. "Do you mean to bid on my bronzes?" He directed the subject-changing question at Giovanni.

"I do," Giovanni admitted, waving his list. "I have been busily copying down numbers."

The gulf between them seemed to be widening. Determined to bridge the gap, Megan strove to find common ground. "I was just saying to Giovanni that a few of your bronzes are not up for auction."

"No," he said, and at last he looked her directly in the eyes again, the intensity of his expression lending added weight to his words. "There are two I could not part with, no matter how dire my circumstances."

In his eyes she saw, unveiled, his troubled hope that she would understand and forgive him his slights. She read, too, a profound sadness touched by fear, even panic, as his gaze roved from her to Giovanni and back again.

"Reed," she said softly, reaching for his hand, hoping in that simple gesture to convey a world of meaning, "you have changed."

He blinked and squared his shoulders, guarding his expression. "Not me, Megan, only my perspective. I ran into Harold Burnham yesterday. He tells me you turned down his proposal of marriage."

"Yes," she murmured, and might have gone on to tell him that he and his mother were convinced she had been posing in the nude for him, if only to relieve some of the seriousness in his expression, had not Giovanni leaned close at that point.

"This must be very difficult for you," he observed.

Reed ran a nervous hand through his hair. "Yes. Wearing in the extreme."

He looked drawn, Megan thought, tired and drawn and yet stronger than she could recall him every having looked before.

"Do you know, there is something profoundly liberating in giving up the trappings of one's life," he said. There was an energy to his statement, a sparkle in his eyes that surprised her, given the circumstances. "My difficulties have forced me to reassess all that I am, all that I value." He looked directly at Megan again, and something in his gaze left her breathless. "I begin to believe these hardships may be a blessing in disguise."

"A blessing?" Megan would never have anticipated such a remark. "What do you mean?"

Reed's attention wavered. Something over her shoulder caught his eye. "Forgive me, but I shall have to explain later. It looks as if the auction is about to begin. Thanks again for coming." He clapped Giovanni on the shoulder and was gone.

Megan wanted to object, to shout out at the injustice of it all—the unfairness. She wanted to sit down in one of Lady Talcott's overstuffed Queen Anne chairs and weep, but she could not, would not break down before the surging crowd of people—each one of whom hoped to carry home a prize with them. Some token of the Talcotts' dispersal of wealth at a fraction of its true value— their good fortune found in another's misfortune.

Feeling dizzy, her stomach in knots, Megan leaned a little heavier on Giovanni's arm and allowed herself to be led inexorably toward the auction hall. The sight of something most unexpected stopped her.

"Are you coming?" Giovanni asked.

Megan let go of his arm, deaf to his question, her eyes locked on a landscape that had been placed in the corner of the room least favorable for viewing. Lot 97, it was labeled. She could not believe her eyes to see it hanging there. With a sense of disbelief she rifled through her auction catalog. Lot number 97, it read, a watercolor landscape, artist unknown, nicely framed.

Numb, Megan backed into Giovanni.

"Megan. Are you all right?" His voice was soft with concern.

"How could he?" she asked breathlessly.

"How could he what?"

"Sell it."

Giovanni, standing behind her, leaned down to her eye level, his cheek brushing hers. "The painting?" he asked.

"Yes."

"There is something special about this painting? I do not recognize the artist, but the frame is very nice."

"Are you sure you do not recognize the artist?" she asked.

He cocked his head, studied the painting intently, let go his hold on her, and crossed the space between them and the watercolor. He turned to look back at her with dismay. "It is yours? The brush stroke and handling of light and shadow looks very much in your style."

"Yes. I painted it. I never dreamed Reed thought so little of it that he would sell it this way."

Giovanni frowned. "I would not have believed Reed Talcott capable of such an ungentlemanly act. But do not despair. I shall buy the painting, no matter the cost."

She tried to respond with a lightness she was far from feeling. "Thank you, Giovanni. I should think it will come cheap in an auction where masterpieces are to be had."

"The true value of art, *cara*, is in the eye of the beholder," Giovanni said, so gently she could not help it, a tear came to her eye.

Chapter Twenty-four

Reed stood beside the podium, watching bidders push into the already crowded auction room. These men and women, he could not help thinking, held his future—the future of is entire family—in their pockets. That they unwittingly wielded such power over him left him with the oddest inclination. He wanted to look each and every one of them in the eyes.

The company was mixed. The Marquis of Stafford was present, along with his good friends the renowned collectors Caleb Whiteford and Julius Angerstein. There was a thick sprinkling of the *beau monde* present and one of Christie's employees was pleased to point out to him a representative for the Prince Regent. George was presently collecting French furniture. There were half a dozen excellent pieces on which his representative was expected to bid.

Oblivious to his intense regard, carefree enough with their responsibility to talk and laugh and enjoy the event, the bidders took position, either seated along benches before the podium, or standing around the perimeter of the room. There, quizzing glasses raised, they continued to examine the enormous oil paintings his father wished to dispose of, in this, the only room with walls of an adequate size for viewing them.

The extensive heights of the ceiling rose in the center of the room to an octagonal tower of sooty, rain-peppered windows that might have allowed light into the room was there any to be had. But there was none. The mood of the weather, in keeping with Reed's own, was decidedly overcast. The rain showed no signs of diminishing. It did, in fact, pelt the windows above him with increasing vigor. Two brass chandeliers had been lit to illuminate the place.

The mass of too many bodies in too-confined a space set the ladies' fans fluttering like birds on the wing. The room began to smell less of beeswax and polish and more of the melange of perfume, pomade, body odor, and wet woolens. The event, he had been informed by an attendant, was far more of a crush than anticipated. The bidding was likely to be quite lively as a result.

At the rostrum, the bookkeeper dipped his pen in readiness. The auctioneer, Mr. Christie the younger, took up the hammer and rapped for silence. Reed's nightmare began in earnest.

Megan sat on one of the hard wooden benches beside Giovanni and stared at Reed as the room fell into an uneasy silence broken only by the buzz of occasional voices, the click of heels on the wooden flooring, the distant scrape and bump of furniture being moved on the floor below, and above everything, the spit of rain on the windows. There was something unreal about the moment, the roomful of people and what they had gathered here to do. Even more unreal was the idea that one of Megan's own watercolors was soon to take its place on the podium, just like the oil that was dextrously removed from the wall and transferred to a stairstep-raised platform where two attendants displayed it on an enormous easel.

The bidders on the benches around her, crowded hip to hip, immediately engaged in an exercise of neck craning. As most of the men did not bother to remove their hats, tricorn or beaver, nor the women their bonnets, a great deal of shifting about was required in order to obtain an unobstructed view.

"Can you see?" Giovanni asked solicitously.

"I see," Megan murmured, her eyes not on the painting but on Reed. *I see*, she thought, *but I do not comprehend*.

From the row in front of them she heard her Aunt Win say to Mrs. Blaynay, "There! That is Reed Talcott. Looking cool as a cucumber. The gentleman in mahogany superfine with the high white stock."

As usual, Reed looked the perfect English gentleman. No different, and yet everything was different. He had taken a seat to one side of the podium. His face was in profile, his attention focused on the painting as the monotonous, repetitive drone of the bidding began.

Megan paid the auctioneer's rattle no mind. The drone of her own repetitive thoughts consumed her. Who was this stranger she had once called friend? Was he the same man for whom she had so long pined? How could he put a price on their friendship? On the expression of her love for him in the gift she had given him? Why would he expose her, through her work, to public humiliation? How could he withhold so much from her, when she had believed he might tell her anything?

The hammer banged down on the auctioneer's podium with the same sharp force of the pain, anger, and hurt she was feeling. Reed Talcott, the cool as a cucumber gentleman in mahogany superfine and the high white stock, whom she had trusted above all others, seemed turned into a monster of sorts, a cruel, unusual, and completely heartless creature.

The auction was an entirely foreign ritual, Reed decided. The regular bidders, as with natives in any foreign country, had a language all of their own. A bored-looking lot, they stood or sat near the podium, evidencing little interest in the proceedings. They exhibited the most profound disinterest when the bids were fiercest. There was a gentleman in the third row, it was whispered to Reed, whose very yawns raised the bid ten percent. The crowd looked, Reed decided, like nothing so much as row upon row of restless children with nervous tics. Clever children, for with the wink of an eye, or the jig of an eyebrow, they meant to win away from him, his life.

Little was said as the bids were made—the room did, in fact, fall into a pensive, rain-battered hush during each negotiation. Even the fans were stilled for fear their movement indicated a bid. Mr. Christie called the going price at an astounding rate when the bids went smartly. A raised eyebrow here, a waggling finger there, an occasional bored wave of an auction guide at the back of the room and the bids rose and rose again until Christie settled the business again and again and again with a smart rap of the hammer.

The oil paintings went, then some of the furniture, brought in one piece after another on the shoulders of four brawny men. A hundred pounds here, seventy-five there, as much as five hundred to pay Talcott debts from the French commode. The bronzes went next, every crack of the hammer a blow to Reed's heart. Then more furniture and china, Lady Talcott's Cortauld silver, Lord Talcott's choicest wines. Pounds, shillings, and pence, the money added up, a long line of scratches from the bookkeeper's pen. All debts would be met. The event might be deemed a unequivocal success. Yet Reed felt diminished with every sale—as if a piece of him were torn away—as if with the sale of every painting a favorite view had been closed away forever from his sight.

With every call for higher bids the dark, rain-pressed sooty closeness of London crowded in on him. The fresh air, open skies, and flowing waters of the Lake District seemed distant indeed. The vistas and views of his very soul seemed threatened. As if to echo the feeling, the rain pelted against the windows above him with increasing energy.

Reed had to remind himself continually of his goals, of his changing perspective, of his hopes for a bright future. The effort of it was exhausting. Even time seemed to flow differently for him in the auction room, as if everything around him sped by at a dizzying rate while his own thoughts and movements had been slowed to a snail's pace.

It was as the watercolors sold that he began to feel light-headed and breathless. Dark spots danced before his eyes. Loath to fall into a dead faint in front of his peers, he moved as inconspicuously as possible to the back of the room, his tally sheet in hand, his self-esteem dragging about his boots. He could no longer bear to face the crowd that bid on his lifetime's accumulation of beloved treasures. It had been hard watching the sale of the bronzes. It was a brutal punishment to see his landscapes lifted to the podium's easel one after another. He halted his retreat near the door.

From this distant vantage point, he could see most of the rostrum and the top half of each painting as it was carried to the display area. Here he could lean against the wall and breathe a bit of fresh air from the doorway. He could hear well enough, too, though the rain seemed bent on reaching a crescendo above them.

Christie had warned him that paintings were not bringing much. "Great Britain has been flooded with French, Belgian, and German collections thanks to Napoleon. Be prepared for the worst."

Reed had believed himself prepared, and the worst was not as bad as it might have been had there been fewer bidders, but to see the Ruisdael go for thirty-five pounds left him speechless. That the authenticity of one of the Poussins should then be questioned by one of the serious bidders right in front of the rostrum and the hammer close on seventy-two pounds, when he had expected it to go for ten times that much, left Reed stricken. Closing his eyes, he braced himself against the wall and reminded himself that the paintings were buying him a slate mine and fruit trees and hops to make beer.

A tap on the shoulder and someone asked in an under-voice, "Are you all right, sir?"

He opened his eyes. One of the attendants, a slender, bespectacled fellow, whose name Reed could not recall, gave him an understanding smile. "How are you holding up? Auctions are generally a nerve-racking experience for those whose goods are involved. An awful sensa-tion—to have strangers haggling over one's things."

"Yes. It is, but I am fine," he said thinly. "No, that's a lie." He pressed his fingers to his temples. "I am any-thing but fine. Completely rattled, in fact. Thank you for asking, Barnaby, is it?"

"Yes, and forgive me if I seem to pry, sir, but have you eaten today?"

"Eaten? I have had the odd bite or two."

"Perhaps a sandwich to take the edge off?"

"Thoughtful of you"—Reed was touched by the man's consideration—"but it would not feel right, leaving."

As if to substantiate his fear, a brilliant flash of light-ening lit up the window-framed sky above their heads. Thunder rumbled the very foundation of the building.

"Five minutes, sir," Barnaby suggested reasonably. "What can five minutes hurt?"

With a sigh, Reed nodded. It would feel good to sit quietly for five minutes to collect himself.

"Lead on then," he said.

Barnaby efficiently beat a path through the crowd to the door, throwing glances over his shoulder now and again to ascertain that Reed was following. The room was jammed, the air had become very close. It was a great relief when at last they broke through the crowd at the door.

Nonetheless, it was with a restless graciousness that Reed accepted Mr. Barnaby's hospitality. "It feels strange," he said as Barnaby poured them each a mouth-ful of brandy and spread a clean bit of paper for the sandwiches. "Strange to sit in a quiet place eating roast beef while within shouting distance my fate is decided by the pounding of an auction hammer and the bored finger waggles of complete strangers."

"I can well imagine." Mr. Barnaby parceled out his sandwiches and waited a trifle expectantly for Reed to partake.

Reed bit into the one that looked like roast beef on a bun. "Mmmm," he said as he chewed vigorously, though the food was completely tasteless to him. "Lovely bread," he said when the bite had been swallowed and sat like a great wad of raw dough in his stomach.

Barnaby smiled. "Fresh bread. Sandwiches are always best when made on fresh bread."

Reed forced himself to bite and chew. He nodded pleasantly at Mr. Barnaby's small talk, but halfway through the bun he rose abruptly, saying, "I do thank you, Mr. Barnaby . . ."

Barnaby rose as well, hastily wiping crumbs from his mouth. "You want to get back, do you?"

"Yes. Am I too predictable?"

"No, sir. Everyone reacts a little differently to the auctions. Some sit in Mr. Christie's office and weep. Some do not participate in the sale at all, their primary interest the money, which they pop by to collect when we are done. But I will not keep you. Would you care to take the rest of the sandwich with you, sir?"

Too touched by his concern to refuse, Reed picked up the remainder of the man's kind offering and bit into the bread and beef more from a sense of duty than appetite. Cheeks bulging, his teeth hard at work, the fresh bread clinging like a limpet to the roof of his mouth, he returned to the auction room. To his surprise, Mr. Barnaby abandoned his fresh bread sandwiches and followed him.

Another watercolor had taken its place on the display easel. Reed could not see from the crowded doorway, but he heard Christie reading the description from the auction guide. ". . . charming watercolor study. Not the work of a master, but nicely framed. The frame itself is worth a starting bid of at least five pounds."

Megan wanted to sink through the floor. *Nice frame?* she wanted to wail. Was that all the man could think of to say about her watercolor. *Not the work of a master!* Of course it was not the work of a master! It was the work of an idiotically infatuated young woman who had foolishly tried to express her love in a sunset view from Yat rock. Megan's skin burned with humiliation, her heart filled with the weight of her anger and anguish.

Beside her, Giovanni leaned forward for a better look at the painting. "This is your painting, is it not?"

Megan nodded. "Yes."

The first half of Reed's beef sandwich had become an indigestible lump in his stomach, the second half, of which he had rashly bitten off more than he could successfully chew, sat like a wad of India rubber in his mouth. He wanted to flee the room again, this time sweeping his treasures into his arms as he went. Which of his lovely paintings was so casually dismissed as of little more worth than the frame it was housed in? Chewing broadly, with the jaw-swinging languor of a cow masticating its cud, he stood on tiptoe to peer between a gentleman wearing a top hat and a woman with too many feathers.

Good God! His sandwich-stuffed mouth dropped open, spilling bits of bread. Megan's watercolor! What in blazes was her painting doing in the bidding? He had no intention of selling her work. How could such a thing have slipped by him?

He wanted to shout, to stop Christie, to inform him the sale of this painting was a mistake, a dreadful mistake—the crowning disgrace in a day of debasement. "No!" he cried at the top of his lungs. But with his mouth still fighting food it emerged a muffled, "Dough."

Mr. Barnaby took a good look at him. "Something wrong, Mr. Talcott?"

"Dat painding ith nod for thale," Reed said, spitting bread.

Barnaby's brows rose. "Not for sale? Are you sure?"

"Yeth."

From the rostrum, Christie was repeating his request for a five-pound bid. "Will no one give me a bid of five?"

Someone near the front took him up on it.

"Dough, dough," Reed shouted, bread still firmly stuck to the roof of his mouth. The gentleman with the top hat turned, frowning, while the woman with the feathers covered her ears with a squeak of protest.

Barnaby tried to deter him as he squeezed between the two. "Not that way, sir! Far too crowded."

Reed ignored him, the only thought in his head to get to the front of the room to halt the sale.

"Will someone give me six?" Christie called.

Reed waved his auction catalog above his head as he wound his way through the press of the crowd. "The painding," he shouted, "ith nod for thale."

Christie seemed unable to hear him above the noise of the rain, but spying the waving catalog, he pointed the hammer in Reed's direction, saying, "The bid now stands at six. We have a rather anxious bidder at the back of the room. Yes, I see you waving, sir."

The crowd chuckled, drowning out Reed's attempt to shout again that the painting was not supposed to be included in the sale.

Dear God! What a nightmare! By his own hand the bid continued! He had to get to the front of the room. He had to get the bread off the roof of his mouth.

"Another bidder," Christie intoned majestically. "We have another bidder. Six pounds two shilling. And another six pounds seven. Anyone care to make it an even seven?"

The bid progressed, no more than a shilling or two at

a time, but faster, nonetheless, than Reed made his way through the crowd. Trapped behind a wall of broad-shouldered young men, he tapped one on the shoulder. "Pleathe, led me path."

The young man turned to face him with an expression of outrage and an overpoweringly rum-scented, "Hands off the coat, if you please."

The wall of backs, four of them, turned. Reed found himself the center of unfriendly attention among the young men, who by their solidarity of spirit would appear to have shared a bottle or two. His polite, "Gennlemen, I musth path," met with a wall of laughter and the suggestion that they should take the rude lisper outside and pummel him.

Megan wanted to throw her skirt over her head and run from the room. The auctioning of her watercolor was an excruciating business. Not only was her poor painting unable to command a decent progression of bids, but the crowd had become so restless some sort of a brew-ha-ha had broken out at the back of the room.

"What is that noise?" Aunt Win leaned back to inquire.

"It is a rudeness," Giovanni replied in a low voice. "This person with the glasses is a rudeness as well." He waved a dismissive hand at the podium, where a bespectacled gentleman was trying to interrupt Mr. Christie's bid announcements. His frantically whispered consultation with one of the attendants in the midst of Mr. Christie's acceptance of another meager raise in the bid won him a frown from the bookkeeper, staying hands from the removers and a severe shake of the head from Mr. Christie himself.

Megan shook her head as well. It was the end of enough, she thought. She would never forgive Reed this humiliation.

Reed succeed in seeing Mr. Barnaby reach the rostrum only because two of the broad-shouldered young men had picked him up with the clear intent of following their harsh words with equally harsh action.

Christie's raised voice stopped them.

"I do beg everyone's pardon," he announced. "It is not at all my custom to interrupt the progress of the bidding once begun, but I have just been informed that this painting is here in error. Mr. Talcott?" He peered out over the crowd, bringing his spectacles down from his forehead in order to do so.

Reed had succeeded in loosening the bread from the roof of his mouth, but it was not so easy to free himself from the gentlemen he had unwittingly offended. As nonchalantly as he could manage with four great beefy hands hoisting him from the floor, Reed waved his auction catalog vigorously and called out evenly, "Here, sir."

"Talcott? Is that you?"

"Yes, sir."

"Will you be so good as to come forward?"

"It would be my pleasure, sir," Reed said. "If these gentlemen will be so good as to put me down."

"Gentlemen?" With a negligent wave of Christie's hand the sea of people parted. A channel opened to the podium.

The rummy mountains had enough of their wits about them to return him to the floor, slightly more rumpled than he had left it. "My thanks, gentlemen," Reed said as he smoothed his coat and set off toward the rostrum, where three bespectacled faces peered intently down at him.

"Is it true, what Mr. Barnaby tells me?" Christie asked in an alarmed undervoice. "You had no intention of selling this painting?"

Reed sighed with relief. "Yes, sir. No intention at all"

Christie leaned over the edge of the rostrum to hold whispered consultation with his bookkeeper. Rain whispered against the windows above. The bidders grew restless and whispered as well. The bookkeeper flipped the pages in his ledger, rifled more pages in the printed catalog, made pencil ticks on each of the pages, and handed the books to Christie, who peered at both entries.

He stabbed at the pages with his forefinger. "My dear Mr. Talcott, it is clearly listed right here, in both books." He waved a hand at the painting. "You see a lot number correctly assigned. We have three bidders currently committed to the purchase of the piece. Unless I am mistaken, you have yourself engaged in the bidding on this piece from the back of the room. Why did you not cry out?"

"What do they say?" Giovanni complained. "Why do they not get on with it?"

"'Tis tedious," Aunt Win said, fanning herself. "It is much too hot for this senseless delay."

Their complaints were echoed on all sides.

Megan burned with anger and humiliation. What was Reed doing now? Was it not bad enough that he was the cause of the fracas at the back of the room? Must he now hold up the bidding she wished more than anything to be finished? Even Christie looked put out with him. He kept shaking his head and pointing to something in his books.

". . . regrettable indeed, you did not succeed in that endeavor," she heard him say.

Regrettable indeed! God help her, she should not have come today.

"I do apologize," Reed said.

Christie was polite but firm. "Your apologies, while welcome, do not change the fact that as gentlemen we can neither of us honorably withdraw from the auctioning of this piece. I am sure you must agree. The bidding is too far engaged."

Reed was not at all inclined to agree.

"Look around you, man," Christie advised him in a whisper. "Should this crowd turn hostile, there is no question life, limb, and property would be endangered. If you are set on keeping the painting, sir, might I suggest you continue trying to outbid the others."

This was not at all the outcome Reed had anticipated, but he had no more than a moment to be stunned. Christie rapped his hammer, consulted the notes before him and announced that the recommencing bid stood at eight pounds eleven. Did anyone care to raise the amount?

Reed turned from the rostrum to a sea of curious faces, his stomach leaden with the undigested truth of what had been said to him on top of stringy roast beef and doughy bread. He had been confident he could halt the sale of the watercolor, confident it, too, could not slip away from him.

"Eight pounds eleven," Christie repeated.

Before Reed could utter a word a familiar voice said firmly, "Eight pounds fifteen."

Giovanni Giamarco sat three rows from the rostrum. Beside him, her face flushed scarlet, sat Megan, her lip caught between her teeth, her eyes downcast. Pain pulled at her mouth. The sight of her knocked Reed unsteady. Lord, what must she be thinking of him in this moment?

It was much easier to read what Giovanni thought of him. He wore an expression Reed had seen before, the same expression with which he had asked on three occasions, pistols, swords, or fists?

"Nine pounds," Reed said softly to the bookkeeper.

Megan looked up swiftly. Nine pounds? Was it really Reed who had just said nine pounds? Pounds he could not afford?

"The bid stands at nine pounds," Christie confirmed,

lifting his hammer, as if prepared to strike the sale closed.

"Nine pounds five shillings," Giovanni's voice seemed too loud, too unbending.

"Ten pounds," Reed's response was as soft as the look in his eyes when his gaze met hers.

"The bid now stands at ten," Christie informed the room. "Ten pounds. Ten pounds going once . . ." The hammer was raised.

Still he stared at her, dear Reed, something in his eyes begging forgiveness. Not a stranger after all.

"Ten and one," Giovanni said evenly.

"Eleven," Reed said gently, beckoning to Giovanni.

Brows raised, Giamarco leaned past several people's heads in the aisle in front of him.

"I never intended to sell this painting," Reed said.

Giovanni smiled, thin-lipped. "I am not the one you should be telling," he said in a low voice, and then, his gaze flickering toward the rostrum, he interrupted Christie's "Going once at eleven, going twice," with the startling bid of, "Fifteen pounds."

"Fifteen pounds," Mr. Christie intoned blandly while a ripple of whispers swept the room.

Giovanni laughed when Reed opened his mouth to increase the bid again, and raised his own bid. "No, double it."

Christie's brows rose. "Thirty pounds, sir, against your own bid of fifteen?"

"Yes," Giovanni assured him. "And my bid goes up ten pounds every time he opens his mouth."

"Giovanni!" Reed and Megan both cried out in astonishment.

"The bid is now forty," Mr. Christie said uncertainly.

There were uneasy murmurs from the crowd.

"Stop this!" Megan tugged on Giovanni's sleeve. "Stop this at once."

"He will be the one to stop it. Not I." Giovanni's eyes glittered with determination. "He does not deserve your painting, any more than he deserves your undying affection. Nor can he afford it. But I can and will take you to Italy with me, one way"—he jerked his head in the direction of the painting—"or another."

Christie was banging down the noise and calling out that the bid stood at forty, as if everyone in the room was not well aware of the fact. "Forty going once, going twice going three times, and . . ."

"Forty-one." Reed's voice stopped the hammer.

"Making the bid now fifty-one to you, sir." Christie waved his hammer at Giovanni.

"Let it go, Reed," Megan called out.

Reed turned to look at her, a long look, his eyes filled with sadness. "It was not supposed to be in the sale, Megan."

"Sixty-one pounds," Christie upped the bid. "Unless you intended every word should be counted, sir?" He asked the question of Giovanni as if such inquiries were nothing out of the ordinary.

"Lord, save me from fools," Megan said softly. Louder she politely begged her aunt's pardon, scandalously hiked up her skirts that she might straddle the bench that separated them, and managed, to the accompaniment of a chorus of "Oh my!" and "How shocking!" and the disapproving tap of her aunt's walking stick, to make her way over yet another bench to Reed. He looked more battered and torn than she could ever recall having seen him. The shoulder seams of his coat were ripped, the fabric severely creased, his eyes and mouth had a tight, tired look, and there were crumbs on his lapel. Poor Reed. Not the English gentleman at all today. "Let it go, Reed," she repeated.

"But . . ."

"Seventy-one pounds," she heard Christie announce blandly.

She placed a finger across Reed's lips to stop him from speaking.

"No buts," she said. "No bids. You cannot afford this madness. This is not a duel. Let the painting go."

She stopped all argument by kissing him.

A gasp went up all around the room, but Megan blocked it from her mind, blocked all but the sensation of her lips against Reed's. She caught him off guard. His mind, it was clear, by the stiffness of his posture, and the rigidity of his response, was on anything but kisses. His initial reaction was to pull away from her unexpected assault.

But Megan gave him no quarter. Gently but firmly she grasped his lower lip between her teeth. Given time, and she was willing to give him time, his mouth softened under hers and his arms stopped their imitation of wood blocks to enfold her in their warmth, even as Mr. Christie hammered down the sale he had been attempting to end for more than half an hour. "Lot number ninety-seven," he called, "going once at seventy-one pounds. Going twice. Three times. Sold, to the gentleman in the third row."

A little cheer went up from the crowd and in the fifth row, as Megan was later informed by her mother-in-law, Lord Talcott made a point of cutting through the crowd that he might lean close enough to Lady Talcott's ear to whisper, "If I bid on your emeralds, my love, is there any chance you might stop me with such a kiss?"

"I would not count on it, my lord," Clarissa Talcott answered coolly. "You could sooner win kisses from me in overseeing the repairs to the road leading up the hill to Talcott Keep."

"It is about time that road had a lasting mend," he had agreed, and for the first time in thirteen years Lord Talcott sat himself down beside his lady wife and took her hand.

Megan's kiss, and it was an incredibly long and involved kiss, came to an end at that point, Megan coming up for air to the accompaniment of a ripple of amused noises from the crowd, and Christie's polite, "Too late for any more bids, Mr. Talcott. You do, I most fervently hope, accept the situation as it now stands?"

Megan smiled up at Reed. "You do," she said.

Reed smiled back at her. "I do," he agreed.

Mr. Christie banged smartly on his rostrum to still the chorus of huzzahs and said politely, his eyes on Giovanni. "I wish you joy in your prize, sir."

Giovanni nodded, directed a courtly bow at Megan and Reed, and thoroughly charmed the crowd, which seemed to wait with baited breath his reaction, in saying, "You will be so good, my dear friends, as to accept this lovely painting as a wedding gift, no?"